LEAVING THE SHALLOWS

Jody could see a gently moving seabed of what looked like green meadow grass, swaying gently in the current.

'These are the seagrass meadows.' Brice appeared beside them. 'There aren't many of them left, so it's up to us to preserve and look after them. They're a very important feeding ground for an endangered species. If we're very lucky, we should see this species. Now be quiet, and watch.'

Jody wasn't sure what they were watching for. But she dutifully stared down into the pale water, and waited.

Suddenly she gave a shout. 'Someone's down there! Someone's fallen overboard!'

Look out for more titles in this series

Summer Specials

Dolphin Diaries™

LEAVING THE SHALLOWS
Lucy Daniels

*Hodder
Children's
Books*

a division of Hodder Headline Limited

Special thanks to Lucy Courtenay

Thanks also to the Whale and Dolphin Conservation Society for reviewing the information contained in this book

Copyright © 2003 Working Partners Limited
Created by Working Partners Limited, London W6 0QT
Text copyright © Working Partners Limited
Illustrations copyright © 2002 Judith Lawton
'Dolphin Diaries' is a trademark of Working Partners Limited

First published in Great Britain in 2003
by Hodder Children's Books

The paper and board used in this paperback by
Hodder Children's Books are natural recyclable products
made from wood grown in sustainable forests. The manufacturing
processes conform to the environmental regulations
of the country of origin.

A Catalogue record for this book is available from the British Library

ISBN 0 340 87383 3

Typeset by Avon Dataset Ltd, Bidford-on-Avon, Warks

Printed and bound in Great Britain by
Clays Ltd, St Ives plc

Hodder Children's Books
a division of Hodder Headline Limited
338 Euston Road
London NW1 3BH

1

March 12 – morning – Pacific Ocean (still).

Everyone got a fright this morning. Out of nowhere, a flying fish landed on the deck with a huge flopping noise, and started thrashing about. It was enormous, with beautiful silvery wings. Everyone yelled and ran around, until Cam managed to scoop it up and throw it back into the sea. I wonder what it was running away from? Something very hungry, I expect!

J ody McGrath closed her diary thoughtfully, and fingered the little silver dolphin she always wore around her neck. The flying fish had been magnificent. The ocean had a habit of throwing surprises at you like that. There was a real mystery about the deep blue water, which Jody knew she'd never fully understand.

Dolphin Dreamer had left the Marquesas Islands in Polynesia four weeks ago. Even after four weeks at sea, the waves still fascinated Jody. Calm one day, and wild the next. Sometimes lit by sunsets and sometimes by moonlight. Jody thought she'd never get bored of looking at them.

She put her diary away, and climbed up into the open air. The decking was warm under her feet and the sun was bright, though the glare from the sea hurt her eyes after the cool of her cabin. She blinked, adjusting to the light. 'Anyone out here?' she asked.

'Yes – and trying to get some peace, *actually*,' came a sarcastic voice.

Jody looked up and saw Brittany Pierce sunbathing on the cabin roof. Brittany was thirteen, and very spoiled. Jody tried hard to like her, but it was difficult. She was so moody! Still, you couldn't really blame her, Jody thought. Her mother had gone to Paris without any warning, and dumped Brittany on

her father, Harry, the captain of *Dolphin Dreamer*.
That had been nine months ago. Brittany had been
much better recently, but the long weeks at sea were
beginning to fray her temper.

'Have you seen Sean and Jimmy?' Jody asked. Her
twin brothers had been making trouble for over a
week. At eight years old, they were not very good at
dealing with boredom.

Brittany groaned. 'Don't ask. They've been
whispering together for the past half hour about
something or other.' She rolled her eyes. 'I mean,
they are *so* immature!' She turned over on to her
front with a sigh.

Jody looked around the deck. Cameron Tucker,
the first mate, was mending a sail. Harry Pierce was
examining a chart.

'Where are we, Harry?' Jody asked, looking over
his shoulder.

Harry smiled at her. 'Miles from anywhere,' he
said cheerfully. 'But we're making good time, given
the distances we've been covering.'

'When will all this sea stop?' Brittany complained.
'I'm sick of staring at waves all day long.'

Harry pointed straight ahead. 'Well, you'll be

pleased to know that we're nearly at the east coast of Australia.'

Australia! Jody thought of all the wonderful marine life that Australia was famous for. Dolphins, sharks, rays – and wonderful coral reefs too.

'Is that where we're going next?' she asked.

Harry looked surprised. 'Haven't your parents told you?'

'I know we're going to Australia,' said Jody. 'I just don't know which part.' She frowned. 'It seems like Mom and Dad haven't decided yet.'

Harry's eyes twinkled. 'I don't blame them. Australia is such a diverse place, especially for marine biologists,' he sighed. 'Choices, choices!'

Jody stared at him. 'But *you* know where we're going, don't you?' she asked suddenly.

'Me?' Harry made a pretence of looking confused. 'I'm just the skipper. I'm quite happy sailing around in circles.'

Jody laughed. 'Very funny!' she joked. 'You know, don't you? Of course you do! Go on, tell me!'

'Go on, Dad,' Brittany added from the cabin roof. 'I need to hear something to cheer me up.'

Harry put his hand on his heart. 'I promised

your mom and dad that I wouldn't breathe a word. You'd better go and ask them yourselves,' he said to Jody.

Jody's heart gave a little skip of excitement. She loved surprises. Just what exactly were her parents planning?

Suddenly she heard Sean's voice. 'Hey, Jimmy!'

Sean was standing innocently on the deck. There was something about his expression which immediately made Jody suspicious.

Jimmy popped up from behind one of the masts. 'Yes, Sean?'

'Have you seen that very big insect lately?' Sean enquired.

Jody frowned. An insect? From her vantage point next to Harry, she could see Brittany's back stiffen at the mention of an insect. She hated insects, as Jimmy and Sean knew.

Jimmy looked interested. 'You mean, that very huge insect we've been talking about?'

Sean nodded his head vigorously. 'I think it's a spider, actually,' he confided. 'It had loads of legs last time I saw it.'

Brittany's back got stiffer.

'It must be very hungry,' observed Jimmy casually. 'After all, we haven't seen land for six weeks. It's probably eaten all the bugs on board already. It'll be looking for food, I expect.'

Jody began to feel worried. A spider? Polynesia had some big spiders, she knew. Could one have got on board without anyone noticing?

'Well,' Sean continued, 'we'd better keep an eye out for it. In case it's dangerous, you know,' he concluded.

Jimmy nodded. 'Definitely,' he said.

Suddenly Sean's eyes grew round. 'There!' he shouted, pointing across the deck. A sprawling, leggy, black shape was lying in the shadow of the main mast.

'Aaaaah!' Brittany shrieked, leaping to her feet. 'A spider! Get it away from me!'

Jody looked closer. The spider didn't seem to be moving. It was lying ominously still. In fact, now that she could see it more clearly . . .

'It's netting!' she exclaimed. 'Just a bit of old black netting!'

Jimmy and Sean exploded with laughter. 'Got you!' they cried gleefully, before giving each other high fives.

Britt gets a nasty surprise

Brittany looked upset. 'I . . . I . . . I think you're awful!' she cried, bursting into tears. 'I hate you!' With that, she fled below deck, sobbing noisily.

'Boys!' Jody said crossly, trying not to smile. 'You know Brittany's scared of spiders. That was really unkind.'

'But it wasn't a real spider,' Jimmy said bluntly. 'It was just pretend.'

'Yes, but Brittany didn't know that,' Jody began.

But Jimmy and Sean were already sidling off. They had spotted Dr Jefferson Taylor snoozing at the far end of the deck. His round red face was covered by his hat, and Jody could hear him gently snoring. Dr Taylor was a scientist who had been sent on this research trip as a representative of PetroCo, *Dolphin Dreamer*'s sponsor.

Somehow, Jody didn't have the heart to stop Jimmy and Sean's fun. She hesitated as she went below, wondering whether to go and check on Brittany, or find her parents so she could ask them where *Dolphin Dreamer* was heading. It was a tough decision.

With a sigh, she turned and knocked at the door of the cabin she shared with Brittany. There was no answer. She knocked again, more loudly this time.

'Go away!' Brittany's voice sounded thick and miserable.

Jody opened the cabin door a fraction. A pillow whistled through the air and crashed into the door, making her jump.

'I said, GO AWAY!' Brittany repeated stubbornly. 'I don't want to talk to you.'

'Jimmy and Sean are just bored,' Jody pointed out. 'They didn't mean any harm. Are you OK?'

Brittany's face crumpled. 'N . . . n . . . no!' she cried, covering her face with her one remaining pillow. 'I want my mom. I hate this stupid ship, and I wish I'd never come!' she finished, turning her face to the cabin wall.

Jody decided to leave Brittany alone for a while and quietly closed the cabin door. She'd have a word with Sean and Jimmy later, and make them apologize. Brittany hated being teased, and would be grumpy for the rest of the trip unless Jody sorted it out.

She wandered down to the office, where she found her mother hunched over the ship's computer. Gina McGrath was often found updating their website, Dolphin Universe, with the latest news on their research trip.

'Come on, Mom,' Jody said immediately. 'The game's up. You know where we're going, Harry said so!' She sat next to her mother. 'Why the big secret?'

Gina grinned. 'How do you know we're going anywhere?' she asked. 'There's plenty of work we could do out here in the ocean, you know.'

Jody opened her mouth to protest, but Gina put a finger to her lips and pointed at the computer screen. It wasn't showing the familiar home page of Dolphin

Universe. Instead, Jody was staring at a photograph of a place she'd never seen before.

Long white sandy beaches stretched away from a beautiful blue sea. Palm trees waved against a deep blue sky. The colour of the water varied from pale turquoise to a deep indigo as the seabed sloped away. With a leap of excitement, Jody realized that this must be their secret destination.

'Come on, Mom,' she begged. 'Where is it? Stop keeping us in suspense!'

Gina scrolled further down the page, coming to a stop on an image of an enormous creature leaping out of the waves with a crash. 'Hervey Bay, Queensland. And this is what Hervey Bay is really famous for,' she said.

'It's a whale!' Jody exclaimed, leaning in closer.

'Hervey Bay is one of the most famous places in the world for whale watching,' said Gina. 'Humpback whales migrate to the warm waters of the bay to escape the harsh Antarctic winter.'

'Wonderful,' Jody breathed. The humpback whale in the picture was *enormous*. She couldn't believe how powerful it must be to leap out of the sea like that. 'Will we see any?'

Gina shook her head regretfully. 'Unfortunately we're too early – or too late, depending on how you look at it. They come to breed between August and October. But Hervey Bay is much more than just a whale-watching site.'

She clicked on another picture, and Jody grinned to see a family of dolphins swimming through the pale, clear water.

'The sea around Hervey Bay is a marine nature reserve,' Gina explained. 'There are dolphins, orcas, rays, dugongs and sharks, among other things.'

Jody stared at the picture. 'So if it's a nature reserve, are they wild dolphins?'

'Yup.' Gina clicked on another image, which showed a female dolphin swimming beside its calf. 'It's amazing, isn't it? And perfect for a holiday!'

A holiday! So *that* was the big surprise!

'You mean, a holiday for us?' Jody asked excitedly.

'Of course.' Gina swung around from the computer screen and took Jody's hands. 'Your dad booked a mooring for *Dolphin Dreamer* last night, in the harbour of Ocean's Point, one of Hervey Bay's best resorts. We didn't want to get your hopes up before we had finalized everything. Don't you think we deserve a holiday?'

Jody thought of the long weeks at sea. She thought about how hard her parents had been working since they had all set off on this research trip last summer, and how wonderful it would be to stay in one place for a little while.

But Jody had one small doubt in her mind. 'No work at all?' she said. She looked at the computer screen again. 'Not even with the Hervey Bay dolphins?'

Gina laughed. 'Do you really think we'd be in Hervey Bay and not visit the dolphins? We couldn't ignore them if we tried! But it'll still be a holiday for everyone. Jimmy and Sean need to work off some steam, and Harry and the crew could use a break. I think you and Brittany could too. What do you think?'

Before Jody had a chance to reply, there was a bellow from the deck, and Dr Taylor flew down the cabin steps at top speed.

Gina leapt to her feet in concern. 'Dr Taylor? Is everything all right?'

Dr Taylor took several deep breaths to compose himself. 'There's a spider on deck,' he managed to gasp. 'I've never seen anything so enormous. I mean,' he amended, 'I'm not afraid of spiders or anything, of course not. But this one is very large. I'm concerned for everyone else . . .'

Jimmy and Sean's laughter floated down into the cabin. Dr Taylor's face coloured to a deep red as he realized that he had been tricked.

Jody turned to her mother. 'I think you're right,' she said. 'We really *could* use a holiday!'

2

March 15 – morning – just off the coast of Ocean's Point, Hervey Bay, Queensland. We've sighted Ocean's Point at last! Just as dawn was breaking this morning, a thin blue line appeared on the horizon. I can see why sailors in the old days used to think they were seeing clouds instead of land – it didn't look real, somehow. Everyone's been talking about Hervey Bay since Mom and Dad broke the news. It sounds like the most incredible place. It's more of a marine reserve than a tourist resort, with lots of important ecological projects going on. Dr Taylor doesn't think we should be having a holiday 'at PetroCo's expense', as he puts it. Dad was very firm with him, *pointing out that we've made good time across the Pacific and we all need a break.*

Jody couldn't tear her eyes away from the coast as *Dolphin Dreamer* finally sailed into the Ocean's Point harbour. Palm trees lined the shore, but in a natural, muddled sort of way, which Jody immediately preferred to all the pictures of expensive, groomed holiday resorts she'd ever seen. Several faded clapboard buildings lined the small harbour, with signs dotted along the pavement advertizing whale-watching trips. The sand on either side of the harbour was almost pure white, and where the water touched the beach, it was so transparent that Jody had to squint to tell where the land ended and the water began.

A shoal of brightly-coloured fish darted under the hull of *Dolphin Dreamer*, following each other's quick movements like a troupe of well-trained ballet dancers. The whole place reminded Jody a little of the Caribbean, where they'd spent some time at the beginning of the research trip. But everything here looked lusher somehow, and rich with the promise of marine life that even the

Caribbean would have found hard to beat.

Away to the left, Jody could see the coast of Fraser Island, stretching back out into the ocean. She'd read that Fraser Island was the world's largest natural island made entirely out of sand. Despite this, it somehow managed to sustain a lush green rainforest and several fresh water lakes. It looked as magical as it had sounded when she'd read up about it on the internet.

'Land at last!' sighed Brittany dramatically. She pulled her sunglasses down from her head and perched them on the end of her nose. 'I need to see different faces before I explode.' She looked across at Jody. 'I guess all you're interested in are the fish,' she said, shaking her head. 'You've got so much to learn, kiddo.'

Jody ignored her, watching as Harry gently steered *Dolphin Dreamer* into her berth. They would be here for a week, and she intended to enjoy every second. Not even Brittany could annoy her now.

'So this is it, is it?' said Dr Taylor fussily. He adjusted his sun hat and peered at the coastline. 'Not much going on.'

Craig McGrath, Jody's father, stepped up on

deck behind Dr Taylor. 'And isn't it wonderful?' he said.

With a gentle splutter, *Dolphin Dreamer*'s engine came to a stop. Harry and Cam leapt down on to the pontoon and quickly fastened the ropes. Suddenly, they were all enveloped in a lovely feeling of calm, with only the gentle sound of lapping water and clinking ropes disturbing the air.

Craig clapped his hands. 'Now we're here, who's for the beach?'

'Me! Me!' Sean and Jimmy hopped around the deck. They were slightly hindered by the flippers and goggles they'd put on first thing that morning, as soon as they'd sighted land.

'I've got some business with the harbour master,' said Harry. 'Don't worry about me.'

Mei Lin, the ship's cook, shaded her eyes to look at the shops along the harbour. 'I need to stock up on a few provisions,' she said. 'After so long at sea, we are really low on everything. Among other things, we could use some fresh fruit – and fresh bread too. I can get a great lunch together, for the first time in weeks!'

Jody's mouth watered at the thought. It had been

so long since she'd tasted warm fresh bread or a sweet juicy orange.

Dr Taylor stood uncertainly on the deck. 'I don't think I'll come to the beach,' he said gravely. 'But a gentle stroll and a leg stretch on the promenade would be quite agreeable, I'm sure.' He looked at the clapboard shops and buildings which stretched colourfully along the harbour front. 'Perhaps I'll be able to pick up some leaflets on marine projects to add to my PetroCo dossier.'

'Good,' said Mei Lin promptly. 'Then you'll be able to help me carry back the food, won't you Dr Taylor?'

Jody stifled a laugh at Dr Taylor's expression. It was clear that his idea of a relaxing walk along the harbour hadn't included carrying back the shopping.

Gina turned to Jody and Brittany. 'Dr Taylor's right about stretching our legs. It'll do us all good to be on land for a change.'

'You bet it will,' said Brittany immediately.

Jody needed no further invitation. She jumped nimbly down on to the pontoon. 'Are you coming, Maddie?' she called over her shoulder.

Maddie was Craig and Gina's assistant, and had been tutoring Jody, Brittany and the boys so that they didn't fall behind on any school work. 'You try and stop me,' she smiled, putting a dollop of sun cream on her slender black legs.

After Cam decided to join the beach party as well, it was quite a sizeable group which made its way up to the harbour front. Jody stared at the local people and holiday makers strolling past. There were lots of different faces, with ruddy tans and freckles. Brittany was right. Much as she loved everyone on board *Dolphin Dreamer*, it was great to see something different for a change.

When they reached the harbour front, Dr Taylor turned to the rest of the group. 'Here is where we part, I think,' he said. 'I'll make my way along the front here, and then head back to the boat. I have some work I should be catching up on.'

Mei Lin raised an eyebrow at him.

'Not forgetting the shopping, of course,' he added with a nervous laugh. 'Enjoy yourselves.'

'Oh, we will,' Gina assured him. 'We most certainly will!'

Jody grinned to herself. Dr Taylor made enjoyment sound like a criminal offence. He was OK once you got to know him, but he always acted rather pompous.

* * *

Jody followed the others towards the beach, walking slowly along the harbour front. The feel of solid ground under her feet was wonderful, though part of her still felt as if she was rocking from side to side. Finding her land legs after four weeks at sea would be a challenge. She found that she had lots of energy, and she wanted to run and shout – just like Sean and Jimmy were doing.

'Why do those little rats have to come?' complained Brittany, as she followed Jody along the harbour front. 'They'll make a horrible noise and probably throw sand around. We won't get a second's peace. It'll be like being on board the boat again.'

'They are only eight,' Gina reminded Brittany as they made their way down a set of rickety wooden steps on to the beach.

'I'm sure I wasn't nearly so much trouble when I was eight,' Brittany muttered.

With a sigh of pleasure, Jody felt the warm, soft sand sliding over the edges of her flip-flops. She kicked them off, and felt the warmth along the whole underside of her foot.

They found a spot under a shady palm tree, where they laid out their towels. Sean and Jimmy immediately tore into the sea with loud whoops.

'Urgh,' said Brittany. She looked around. 'I'm going to sunbathe on that rock over there,' she said at last, indicating a smooth dry rock sticking out into the sea. 'Away from the sand, and away from the *kids*.'

Jody watched Brittany walk carefully along the beach and make her way out to the rock. She hadn't even taken off her flip-flops.

'Don't forget to use lots of cream!' Gina called after her. 'The sun gets so hot, you can't be too careful,' she said worriedly. 'Do you think she'll be all right?'

Maddie took off her sundress and straightened the straps of her costume. 'Don't worry, Gina,' she said. 'I'll go for a swim by the rock, and keep an eye on her. It's only nine-thirty – the sun isn't too hot at the moment. Brittany is too sensible to burn.'

And too vain, thought Jody with an inward grin.

'I'll join you, Maddie,' Cam said.

The water looked inviting, particularly when the

sun shone through the sparkling droplets which flew up as Cam dived in. Jody stared thoughtfully at the gleaming waves.

'Go on, then,' said Gina, noticing her daughter's expression. 'Go and have a swim. Just stay where we can see you, OK?'

The sea was just as cool as Jody had hoped. She waded out into deeper water, and dived down below the surface. Twisting and turning like a fish, she savoured every second of it. When she surfaced at last, and floated calmly on the top of the water, Jody decided that she'd never felt so relaxed in her whole life.

She heard a familiar clicking sound somewhere on her right. Immediately alert, she looked around expectantly. Dolphins! This was her lucky day. She hadn't expected to see them so soon.

About five metres further out to sea, the water heaved, and Jody gasped with delight to see a waving flipper breach the surface of the water. With a powerful beat of its tail, the dolphin leapt into the air. After its somersault, it cut cleanly back into the water again.

Although it had a slender bottle-shaped beak, Jody

Floating peacefully!

knew immediately it wasn't a bottlenose – the colouring looked wrong. So what was it?

Jody paddled a little to one side so that she was facing in the right direction, in case the dolphin reappeared. She knew that you should never approach a wild dolphin, and she was careful to keep her distance.

The dolphin emerged again and floated for a moment on the surface of the water, breathing gently through its blowhole. Jody was intrigued to see that it had a curious outline, with a pronounced bump on its head and a strange, fatty hump just below its fin. It was an unusual colour, too – splashed pink and white.

The dolphin dipped below the surface of the water again, and Jody watched the water ripple away in its wake. Intrigued, she sculled gently around the area on her back. Would it come back a third time?

'Hey!'

Startled, she turned around to see a figure swimming towards her. When he stopped to tread water, Jody saw from his dark green armband that he was one of the wardens she had noticed on the beach earlier. He had an anxious expression on his face, which made Jody's stomach turn over.

'Stay exactly where you are!' he shouted. 'Don't move, OK?'

Jody froze. She knew the tone of his voice meant something serious. And the first thing she thought was – *sharks*!

3

'Can you move away from the dolphin, please?' the warden asked, when he finally reached Jody.

'Where's the shark?' Jody said anxiously, looking all around her.

The warden looked surprised. 'Shark?' he said. 'There's no shark. Just you and a dolphin. I need you to move away, please.'

With a rush of relief, Jody realized what had happened. There was no shark! She started giggling – she couldn't help it.

'It's no laughing matter,' said the warden sternly, a

perplexed frown crossing his tanned face. 'Approaching wild dolphins can be really dangerous.'

Jody laughed helplessly. 'I'm sorry,' she managed to gasp. 'I thought there was a shark. I thought you were coming to rescue me!' Then, because of the shock, she dissolved into laughter again.

At last she gained control of herself. 'I'm really sorry,' she said again. 'It's just that I would never in a million years approach a wild dolphin. I've grown up with dolphins, you see. I know the rules.'

Jody swam back into shore with the warden, who introduced himself as Brice. It seemed that he worked at Ocean's Point, running tours and keeping an eye on things, along with his boss David.

'So what brings you here?' Brice asked when the water became shallow enough to walk.

Jody explained all about *Dolphin Dreamer* and her parents, and how she'd spent the past nine months travelling around the world and visiting research sites in the Caribbean, South America and Polynesia.

Brice clapped his hand to his forehead. 'I've heard about you guys!' he said. 'My boss got an email from your dad, now I come to think about it.'

'Dad can't resist contacting fellow dolphin fans, even when we're on holiday!' Jody laughed as they waded back on to the beach. The sand felt doubly hot after the coolness of the water.

'So what do you think of Ocean's Point and your holiday so far?' asked Brice, combing a hand through his tangled blond hair.

Jody thought about how calm she had felt as she watched the strange pink and white dolphin leaping out of the water. 'Wonderful,' she said honestly, looking back out to sea.

'That was Dawn you saw out there,' Brice said, pointing back out to sea. 'Her Latin name is *sousa chinensis*, although she's better known as the speckled or Indo-Pacific humpbacked dolphin.'

'A humpbacked dolphin?' Jody remembered the strange bump on Dawn's back. 'I didn't know there were humpbacked dolphins as well as humpback whales. Are they rare?'

'We don't know exactly how many humpbacks are out there,' said Brice, 'but we do know that they divide into two types. In the western Pacific, they usually have a hump. In the east, they don't, but they have a taller fin. Dawn is the first type, as you probably saw.'

'Do people ever mistake them for bottlenoses?' Jody asked, remembering Dawn's slender beak.

'Sometimes,' replied Brice. 'But only at first glance. Because when you get up close, you can see how different their shape and colouring is from the bottlenose. They come in pink or grey, or various shades in between. There's even a colony in Hong Kong which is almost completely white!'

Jody was intrigued. 'Do they like people?'

'They aren't that sociable as a rule,' said Brice. 'They don't like boats, and are much slower in the water than bottlenoses, so don't tend to bow-ride.'

'But Dawn came in really close to the shore,' Jody pointed out. 'And she wasn't afraid of me. You saw her – she was almost as near to me as you are now!'

'Humpbacked dolphins always feed in shallow water, so they know about people and coastal development,' explained Brice. 'But strangely, they are well known for being difficult to approach. I think Dawn is the exception to the rule. She's a big fan of the tourists.' He paused. 'In fact,' he added slowly, 'sometimes I think she likes tourists a bit too much.'

Jody was surprised. 'In what way?'

Brice looked thoughtful. 'She's a regular at Ocean's Point, and I've noticed that she's been putting on weight. It wouldn't surprise me if she was finding food somewhere she shouldn't.'

'Where?'

Brice swept out a strong, tanned arm, indicating the coastline. 'This part of Queensland has plenty of tourist resorts,' he said. 'Some of them actively encourage dolphins to swim into shore to interact with visitors.'

Jody couldn't believe her ears. 'Wild dolphins?' she asked.

'Technically wild,' said Brice with a frown. 'But increasingly reliant on handouts. It's not something we encourage at Ocean's Point.' He smiled at her. 'As you've just seen.'

'Who's your friend, Jody?' Gina approached them, flip-flops in hand.

Jody waved her dad over as well and made some introductions. As ever, Craig and Gina were happy to meet a fellow dolphin enthusiast, and were soon eagerly discussing their worldwide project with Brice. Jody left the adults to chat for a while. She walked over to her brothers, who were scuffling in the sand.

'So how many disasters have you two caused so far, then?' she asked.

Jimmy looked indignant. 'Apart from splashing that family over there and kicking sand in that lady's picnic by mistake, we've been really good,' he declared.

'And you hit that man with the frisbee,' Sean pointed out.

'Only because you said I wouldn't be able to,' Jimmy protested.

Craig moved away from Gina and Brice, and came towards them. 'They've tired me out anyway, I can tell you,' he smiled, putting Sean in a friendly headlock. 'How was the sea?'

'Great!' Jody enthused. 'And I saw a dolphin!'

'So I heard.' Craig looked amused. 'They always seem to know when you're around, Jody!'

Jody told him all about her close-up experience with Dawn.

'I haven't seen an Indo-Pacific humpbacked dolphin for years,' said Craig thoughtfully. 'I'd like to take a look. Brice told me that several feed in these waters.'

'Maybe she'll come back again,' Jody said hopefully.

'Let's hope so,' Craig said. 'Brice did say that she was a regular.' He released Sean and clapped his hands. 'Come on, guys. Our new friend Brice here has invited us back to HQ, to tell us a bit more about the resort and Hervey Bay.'

Jody shaded her eyes and checked the position of the sun. It was getting quite high. She knew that staying outside in the middle of the day wasn't a good idea. A quick trip to Brice's cool shady office would be very welcome.

'Coming?' Craig asked.

'Will there be ice creams?' asked Jimmy cunningly.

'Maybe,' said Craig. 'But only if you pack up your beach things in exactly ten seconds flat!'

Craig, Gina, Brice, Jody and the boys made their way down to the waterfront. They could see Brittany still sunbathing on the rock at the far end of the tidebreak.

'Brittany!' called Gina. 'We're going into town. I'd rather not leave you here on your own, so you'd better come with us. We'll come back to the beach later.'

Brittany sat up and adjusted her sunglasses. Even at this distance, Jody could tell that she wasn't very pleased at being disturbed.

'I want to stay here!' she complained. 'I'm just starting to get a tan. Anyway, if I go now, I'll lose this sunbathing place.'

'Brittany sweetheart, we haven't got time to argue—' Gina began.

'I'm not a baby,' Brittany interrupted hotly. 'I can look after myself, you know.'

'We can stay with Brittany,' Maddie offered, wading out and shaking the water from her ears. 'Cam's not going anywhere either. Look at him!' She pointed at the figure fast asleep on a brightly-coloured lilo, which was bobbing gently in the shallows.

'Thanks Maddie,' said Gina gratefully. 'Just try and get Brittany into the shade some time soon. It's approaching eleven o'clock, and I don't want her going down with heatstroke.'

Jody saw her mother look at the jagged rocks of the tidebreak.

'And could you keep an eye on her if she goes anywhere near those rocks?' Gina added. 'If Brittany slips and falls in, it could be nasty.'

'She'll be fine,' Maddie insisted. 'Go and have fun! We'll see you later.'

The Ocean's Point wardens' office was a whitewashed wooden hut at the far end of the harbour, above a small jetty, where a gleaming launch boat, called *Kookaburra*, lay at a mooring.

What a boat!

Brice unlocked the office door, and ushered everyone into the shady interior. A fan was whirring energetically on the wall, filling the room with a welcome breeze. 'My boss is over on Fraser Island today with a four-wheel drive tour,' he explained. 'But I know he'd love to meet you some time.'

'We'd like that,' said Craig. 'The four-wheel drive tour sounds fun too. Do you have many activities around here?'

'Lots,' Brice laughed. 'As well as the four-wheel drive tour, there are sailing trips, fishing trips, and quad bikes.'

Jimmy and Sean looked up from their melting chocolate cones at the mention of quad bikes.

'Everything is carefully monitored, though,' Brice continued. 'We don't want to ruin the natural environment. There aren't many places left like Hervey Bay and Fraser Island, so we've got to look after them.'

Brice quickly fell into a long and detailed conversation about the environmental projects of Hervey Bay and Fraser Island with Craig and Gina, leaving Jody to keep an eye on her brothers. They had now finished their ice creams and were looking for new distractions.

'Check this out!' Jimmy pointed at a glossy poster of Pacific marine life, which was pinned to the office wall.

'Cool,' Sean agreed, peering closely.

'I've got an idea,' said Jody. 'I'll give you two minutes to stare at this poster, and then I'll ask you to write down the names of all the animals you can remember. The person who remembers the most wins, OK?'

Jimmy cocked his head. 'Wins what?'

'The best prize in the world,' said Jody. 'The pleasure of beating your brother and then boasting about it for a few days.'

'Excellent!' shouted Sean.

While her brothers were memorizing the poster, Jody read the leaflet pinned up next to it. It was a flyer all about the history of Hervey Bay. It had been discovered by Captain Cook while travelling down the east coast of Australia, and he'd named it after his boss, Lord Augustus Hervey. He hadn't been very thorough, Jody decided. He'd called it Hervey *Bay* because he'd thought Fraser Island was joined to the mainland. She traced the outline of Fraser Island on the large wall map next to the office door. If Captain Cook had travelled a little further south, he'd have discovered the narrow strait of water which separated Fraser Island from the rest of Australia.

Jody checked her watch. 'Right, time's up!' she said to the twins. 'Let's ask Brice for some paper and a couple of pens.'

Jody's parents and Brice stopped their conversation, and Brice found something for the boys to write on. Soon Jimmy and Sean's chatter gave way to the sound of busy scribbling.

'You're good at entertaining your brothers,' Brice commented, smiling at Jody.

'They've been running around the beach all morning, so getting them to sit still now is easy,' said Jody. 'There isn't any room on board *Dolphin Dreamer* for running around, so it's much harder keeping them out of trouble then.'

'They love it here,' said Gina, joining in the conversation. 'Ocean's Point gives them plenty of space – and gives the rest of us a break!'

'Kids sometimes find Ocean's Point too quiet,'

Brice said. 'Families often prefer the amusement arcades and fun fairs of the resorts further south.'

'You said something about the resorts in the south earlier,' said Jody, remembering.

Brice nodded. 'Yes, as I said, there are quite a few. Parts of the coast are getting pretty overdeveloped now.'

'Is that a problem for the wildlife?' Craig asked with a frown.

'It used to be pretty bad in the past,' said Brice. 'You heard about tourists encouraging dolphins to swim close into shore, where they would beach themselves and then be unable to get back into the sea. Because of too much uncontrolled human contact, some dolphins would stop feeding their own young and become unusually aggressive. I even heard of dolphins catching quite nasty human diseases.'

'That's horrible,' said Jody with feeling. She thought of Dawn.

'You can see why I'm worried about Dawn,' Brice said, reading Jody's expression. 'The only good news is that over-exploitation is much less common than it used to be. These days, we keep accurate records of visiting marine life, so we can pinpoint problems pretty quickly. We also do whale-watching boat trips in season, and trips out to the seagrass meadows and into deeper waters the rest of the year. We prefer to take the visitors to the wildlife, not the other way round. That takes some of the pressure off the coastline, and discourages dolphins from coming too close to shore.'

He pointed outside, towards the wooden jetty. 'You probably saw our tour boat, *Kookaburra*, moored out there. And there are other places like Ocean's Point along this coast which operate on similar principles.'

He paused. 'But on the other hand, there are still places along this coast with serious problems,' he admitted. 'If we could keep the dolphins at Ocean's Point, we'd be able to protect them. But they are wild creatures, and we don't believe in penning them in.'

Jody jumped at a sudden crash in the corner of the office. She swung around.

'Jimmy!' cried Gina, throwing her hands in the air.

Jimmy stood next to the overturned office chair,

whose wheels were gently spinning in the air. A wastepaper bin also lay on its side, spilling a fluttering heap of paper across the floor.

'It was Sean,' he said unconvincingly.

'I think we'd better take the boys back to *Dolphin Dreamer*,' Craig apologized to Brice. 'Before they break something.'

Brice laughed. 'But I haven't shown you around *Kookaburra* yet!' he said. 'Maybe you'd like to come out on a trip this afternoon?'

'We'd love to!' Jody said enthusiastically. She had totally fallen in love with this place, and couldn't wait to explore it further. 'Dad, can we?'

'I don't see why not—' Craig began.

There was another crash as the office door flew open, letting in a flood of light. Maddie stood framed in the doorway.

'Is Brittany here with you?' she asked urgently.

There was a pause.

'We left her with you!' Gina exclaimed.

Maddie looked anxious. 'I know. One minute she was there, and the next she was gone. If she isn't here with you, where can she have got to? I've looked everywhere for her.'

41

'Did you check *Dolphin Dreamer*?' asked Craig.

Maddie nodded unhappily. 'Harry hadn't seen her. He's out looking for her on the beach now.'

'We'd better join the hunt,' said Gina. 'Brice, it's been a pleasure talking to you. Now we'd better go and find Brittany.'

4

'Don't worry, Gina,' said Maddie. 'Wherever Brittany is, I'm sure she's fine. She took her towel with her, so she must have wandered off somewhere on purpose.'

'She should have said something to you,' sighed Gina, passing a hand over her forehead. 'Now we'll have to spend ages looking for her, and I know Mei Lin is expecting us back on board for lunch soon. Honestly. This is supposed to be a holiday!'

'I'm sure you'll find her,' said Brice reassuringly, locking the office door behind him. 'Why don't you come back after lunch? I meant what I said about giving you a look around *Kookaburra*. We've got a tour at two o'clock, if you're interested. Maybe see you later?'

'Thanks,' Gina nodded. 'If we can make it, that would be great.'

There was no sign of Brittany at the beach.

'You two go that way,' Craig instructed Maddie and Cam, pointing away from the harbour front. 'We'll check out the harbour. Let's meet back at the jetty in half an hour, OK?'

Jody went with her parents to the harbour front, where they asked every passer-by whether they'd seen a girl on her own with wavy fair hair and pink flip-flops.

'We'll check inside the shops, and you stay out here, Jody,' Gina said at last. 'She must be around somewhere. We'll see you at the jetty.'

Several times, Jody thought she'd spotted Brittany in the crowd, but it always turned out to be someone different. With a sigh, she turned her attention to the small waterfront café on the harbour front.

Jody suddenly spotted Dr Taylor sitting at one of the café chairs.

Dr Taylor looked a little embarrassed. 'Ah, hello Jody,' he said, pushing his large ice-cream sundae to one side. 'Just a quick break, you know.' He patted a small pile of leaflets on the table. 'Thirsty work, research!' he added jovially. 'Now, is something the matter?'

Jody explained about Brittany. Dr Taylor nodded carefully. 'Yes,' he said at last. 'That doesn't surprise me. She certainly is a wilful young lady.'

'Have you seen her?' Jody persisted.

Dr Taylor shook his head. 'No,' he admitted. 'I've been reading these leaflets, you see. One hundred per cent concentration needed!'

'There you are, Dr Taylor!' Jody heard Mei Lin's voice, and turned around to see the slender Chinese woman standing with her arms full of grocery bags. 'Are you ready to go back to the boat? There are several more of these to collect,' she added meaningfully, indicating the small mini-market a hundred metres away.

Dr Taylor grumbled under his breath, before heading in the direction Mei Lin was pointing.

'Mei Lin, have you seen Brittany?' Jody asked hopefully.

Mei Lin shook her head. 'I know Maddie was looking for her earlier, because she came back to *Dolphin Dreamer* and told us,' she said. 'So you still haven't found her?'

Jody shook her head.

'Don't worry,' said Mei Lin comfortingly, hefting her groceries into a better position. 'It's nearly twelve o'clock. Brittany won't miss lunch! I'll see you back at the boat in no time.'

After half an hour, Jody gave up, and started hurrying back to the jetty to meet the others.

'So that's why it's called Hervey Bay . . .'

Jody stopped as she heard a very familiar voice behind her.

'Brittany!' Jody swung around in relief to see Brittany strolling along with a tall, tanned boy in sunglasses. 'There you are! We've been looking everywhere for you!'

'Why? What's all the fuss?' Brittany looked perplexed. She turned to her companion. 'I just hooked up with Jason here, and we got talking.'

Gina and Craig came running up. 'There you are!' cried Gina in relief. 'Brittany, where on earth have you been?'

Brittany looked mutinous. 'I was just talking to Jason,' she said.

'You should have told Maddie or Cam where you were,' Craig said crossly. 'We've been worried sick.'

Brittany rolled her eyes at her companion. 'It's my holiday too. I am thirteen, you know. Mom always lets me go off on my own.'

'Still, you should have told someone where you were going,' Craig repeated. He turned to Jason. 'Will you excuse us? Brittany has some explaining to do.'

Jason shrugged. 'No worries,' he said, before walking off towards the beach.

Brittany glared. 'That was so embarrassing,' she muttered.

'Embarrassment is the least of your problems,' said Craig severely. 'I think your dad might have something to say about this. It's time to head back to *Dolphin Dreamer* for lunch.'

He paused, looking at Brittany's face. 'And by the way,' he added grimly, 'your nose is going to peel.

March 15 – lunchtime.
Brittany has shut herself in our cabin, and is refusing to

speak to anyone. I think it's partly because she's in a sulk, and partly because she doesn't want anyone to see her bright red nose. She didn't have enough suncream on after all. I suppose you can't really blame her for wanting to do her own thing. I think the big mistake was not telling anyone where she was going.

Now we've found her, it means that we can go back to the wardens' office after lunch, for a deep-sea tour aboard Kookaburra! *Maybe we'll see Dawn again? Even if we don't, I know we're going to see some amazing things.*

Lunch was fantastic. As Jody sank her teeth into fresh, juicy tomatoes and crunched through crisp salad leaves, she thought she'd gone to heaven.

'How did old-time sailors survive whole *months* at sea?' she asked Harry as she bit hungrily into another fluffy, poppy-seeded bread roll.

Harry laughed. 'With great difficulty,' he joked. 'I'm pleased to say that I've never been at sea for more than a couple of months at a time, so I've never had the pleasure of weevil-infested biscuits and rotten meat.'

'Yuk!' said Jimmy. 'Did they have to eat the ship's rats too?'

Jody noticed that Brittany wasn't eating very much. She was picking quietly at a roll and staring at the deck. Jody guessed that Harry had said a few harsh words to his daughter when they'd got back on board.

'More cheese, Brittany honey?' Gina gently offered Brittany the plate. 'Mei Lin found some lovely fresh cream cheese for us.'

Brittany pushed her chair back. 'I'm sorry, OK?' she blurted out. 'I should have told you I was going. I was just . . .' She paused, struggling for words. 'I just needed to get away from everyone for a bit . . .' She stopped abruptly.

Craig put his hand on her shoulder. Brittany always found apologizing very hard to do. 'That's OK,' he said quietly. 'Don't worry about it.'

Brittany looked across at Jody, her eyes brimming with tears. 'Is my nose really bad?' she asked in a watery voice.

Jody thought Brittany's nose was redder than the tomato on her plate, but she wasn't going to say that. 'No,' she lied. 'It'll be fine. Just put lots of sunblock on it and stay out of the sun for a bit.'

Brittany sniffed and picked up the remains of her

roll. She didn't say another word at lunch, and as soon as the plates were cleared, she disappeared into her cabin.

'Isn't Brittany coming with us on the *Kookaburra* tour?' Jody asked, watching Brittany go.

'She's feeling a bit sorry for herself today,' said Harry, folding away the lunch table and stowing it neatly. 'I think she just needs a bit of time. I'm sure she'd love to hear about it later, Jody.'

'So you'll have to remember all the smallest details for her,' Gina advised.

'I'll remember those anyway,' Jody said honestly.

'Shame you don't remember your maths formulae quite so easily!' remarked. Maddie with a grin.

Jody, her brothers and her parents made their way to the Ocean's Point wardens' office at a quarter to two. Brice was waiting for them.

On closer inspection, *Kookaburra* turned out to be a catamaran with a special glass floor, so visitors could see under the water. Even moored at the jetty, Jody was enthralled by the view through the glass. She could see seaweed waving on the ocean bed, and shells on the seabed floor.

Kookaburra was painted blue and white, and built on three levels. There was a sea-level viewing platform, with the glass floor inside and an open deck at the front of the boat. The second level was completely covered, allowing viewing and seating, and finally there was the cockpit at the top. Jody and the twins explored every inch, delighting at the framed pictures of whales and dolphins on the walls, and the twisting stairways which took them from level to level.

'Hey!' a timorous voice called from the jetty. 'Is anyone aboard?'

Jody ran out on deck. 'Brittany!' she said in delight. 'You came!'

Brittany stood sheepishly on the jetty, clutching a small beach bag. She was wearing a large floppy sun hat, and her nose was liberally coated in white sunblock. She twisted her hair around her fingers. 'Can I come on the tour?' she asked tentatively.

'Of course you can, honey,' said Gina warmly, holding out her hand to help Brittany step aboard. 'Good to have you with us.'

Brittany immediately wanted to go right to the top deck.

Brittany tries to make amends

'There's not much to see up here,' Jody said, when they got there. 'Wait till you see *Kookaburra*'s glass bottom – it's amazing!'

Brittany slowly looked around the tiny top deck. 'I like it up here,' she said. 'I want to look at the view.' She leaned on the rail and gazed back towards the harbour and the beach.

Something about the expression on Brittany's face made Jody wonder if she was looking for someone. 'Did that boy say he was coming on the tour?' Jody said, with a sudden flash of inspiration.

Brittany flushed a dark red. 'He may have done,' she said in a careless voice. 'I can't remember. I didn't talk to him for long.'

'Talk to who?' Jimmy poked his head up the steps.

Brittany stared desperately at Jody. She obviously didn't want Jody to say anything about the boy at the beach.

'Talk to Brice of course,' Jody said. 'Who do you think?'

Jimmy shrugged, bored with the conversation already. 'Sean just saw an octopus through the glass bottom of the boat,' he declared, and disappeared down the steps again.

'Thanks, Jody,' said Brittany gratefully. 'I owe you one. If Jimmy knew I'd been talking to a boy, he'd only make a big thing of it.' She looked across at the beach again.

'Is that him?' asked Jody suddenly.

A tall boy was walking down the jetty, towards the boat.

'Yes!' Brittany squealed, turning red again. She swung around to Jody anxiously. 'My nose doesn't look too awful, does it?'

'Aussies always wear stripes of sunblock on their

noses,' Jody said generously. 'I'm sure Jason will think it's cool.'

At two o'clock exactly, *Kookaburra* pulled away from the jetty, and headed out into the open sea. Brittany and Jason had immediately got talking, and now they were sitting together at the front of the boat with their heads together.

'Welcome aboard the *Kookaburra*, folks.' Brice's voice sounded over a loudspeaker. 'Let's go and see what Hervey Bay has to offer!'

The next hour passed like a dream for Jody. She stood at the bow, holding on tightly to the rail. It wasn't long before the first dolphins made an appearance, leaping high off to starboard.

'Bottlenose dolphins are quite common in these parts,' Brice's voice stated. 'But you need to keep your eyes peeled for their shyer cousins, the Indo-Pacific humpbacked dolphin. We have some visitors aboard who know more about dolphins than I do, and I'm sure they'll be happy to answer your questions – Craig and Gina McGrath, from Florida!'

The other tourists looked curiously at Craig and Gina, and Jody felt a stab of pride.

Pelicans came into view, flying in low, ungainly swoops along the water. The baggy sacs in their bills meant that they could scoop unsuspecting fish clean out of the water, and either swallow them direct or save some for later.

'These waters are teeming with fish, as you might expect,' Brice's voice continued, as *Kookaburra* began to leave the deep water behind and head for the shore of Fraser Island. 'Species include snapper, coral trout, bream, sweetlip and trevally, plus others such as tuna, mackerel and marlin. All good feeding for our friends the pelicans, and the ospreys which nest on the mainland.'

Jody saw a humpback shape break the surface of the water briefly, and then disappear. She turned to Brittany. 'Did you see that?' she said in excitement.

Brittany looked up from her conversation with Jason. 'See what?' she said.

'I'm sure that was a humpbacked dolphin,' explained Jody, turning back to the sea again. *Maybe it was Dawn*, she thought to herself. She craned her neck in case the dolphin reappeared, but there was no sign.

Brice brought the *Kookaburra* about half a mile from the shore of Fraser Island, and dropped anchor in the clear waters of a sheltered bay. The sandy, tree-tangled shore looked wild and uninhabited, but the waters were quite the opposite. The water here was perfectly clear, with a light aqua tinge. Jody could see different shapes and colours as a large turtle swam past and small fish darted around in the shallows.

'It's a bird!' Brittany cried in astonishment, as a gliding shadow seemed to fly along beneath them, beating strong wings.

Sean and Jimmy laughed.

'That's a manta ray, Brittany,' Gina said gently. 'Though to be fair, it does look like a bird when it flies along like that.'

'I thought it was some kind of bird too,' said Jason gallantly.

Brittany blushed, and put some more sunblock on to her nose.

Jody could see a gently moving seabed of what looked like green meadow grass, swaying gently in the current.

'These are the seagrass meadows.' Brice appeared beside them. 'There aren't many of them left, so it's up to us to preserve and look after them. They're a very important feeding ground for an endangered species. If we're very lucky, we should see this species. Now be quiet, and watch.'

Jody wasn't sure what they were watching for. But she dutifully stared down into the pale water, and waited.

Suddenly she gave a shout. 'Someone's down there! Someone's fallen overboard!'

5

Brice raced up beside Jody. 'Where?' he said urgently.

Jody pointed down into the water with a shaking hand. Whoever it was wasn't moving. Were they dead already?

Brice stared down into the water. Then he burst out laughing.

'It's OK, folks,' he called back to the other tourists, who had gathered around the edge of the boat. 'No one's in danger. In fact, what we're looking at here is a wonderful sight. Someone tucking into a hearty meal!'

Jody stared. The 'person' had started moving. It changed position and brought its head down to the seagrass, where it calmly began to graze.

'What is it?' asked Brittany, hanging back fearfully.

'It's a dugong,' replied Craig, putting his hand on Jody's shoulder.

A dugong? Jody remembered reading about dugongs when she had first looked at the Hervey Bay website. Her heart stopped racing, and she started feeling rather stupid.

'Sailors used to mistake dugongs for humans,' said Brice kindly. 'Well,' he amended, 'not humans exactly. But sirens, or mermaids.'

'Mermaids?' Jimmy echoed, peering over the edge of the boat. 'That's a seriously ugly mermaid!'

The dugong wasn't the prettiest creature Jody had ever seen. It was enormous, with a wrinkled hide and stout, powerful flippers. Its snout was blunt and whiskered. Jody watched as it rooted gently along the seabed, tearing up the seagrass and munching slowly.

'Because they feed almost exclusively on seagrass, they're also known as sea cows,' explained Brice.

'Cow is a bit more realistic than mermaid,' snorted

Brittany. 'Those sailors must have been pretty stupid.'

Brice smiled. 'Mermaids were said to lure ships on to dangerous rocks, and drive men mad with their seductive songs. The sailors were probably too superstitious to look too closely. When you've been at sea for several months, your water and your food is low. If your ship is straying dangerously close to the shore, maybe you'd think these creatures were mermaids too.'

Brittany tossed her head. 'As if!' she said scornfully.

'I think they're pretty cool,' said Jason.

'I'm not saying they aren't *cool*,' said Brittany, glancing at Jason. 'They just aren't mermaids, that's all.'

Jody leant further over the rail, and squinted down into the glittering water to get a better look at the dugong. 'How big do they grow?' she asked.

'This one's a young male – he looks to be about two and a half metres long. But they can grow up to three metres,' Brice said. 'That's roughly twice the height of your mom.'

Jody glanced across at her mother, who was deep in conversation with an American couple on the deck. The image of a dugong standing on its tail and towering over Gina made her smile.

'They can live for a long time, about seventy years or so.' Brice leaned on the *Kookaburra*'s railings and watched the dugong as it grazed peacefully below them. 'But they don't start breeding until the females are roughly ten to seventeen years old. They only have one calf every three to five years, and pregnancy lasts thirteen months. So the population doesn't increase as fast as we'd like it to.'

'You said they were an endangered species,' Jody recalled aloud. 'Is that because they don't breed fast enough?'

'Partly that,' said Brice. 'But mainly because there aren't many seagrass meadows left. When you think that a full-grown adult dugong will put away around twenty-five kilograms of seagrass a day, that's a whole lot of food. Maintaining the seagrass meadows is one of the main projects we have in Hervey Bay. If we don't look after the meadows, we'll lose these amazing creatures for good.'

As she talked to Brice, Jody learned more about dugongs. Although they looked like very heavy dolphins or seals, their closest relative was the elephant. And unlike dolphins or whales, they couldn't hold their breath for much longer than fifteen minutes at a time – or less, if they were swimming fast.

'So we should see this one surface?' Jody asked hopefully.

Brice nodded. 'Should do. Unless he chooses to swim further away from the boat before he takes a breather.'

There was a shout from the other side of the boat. Dolphins!

'There's a group of four just to the seaward side of us,' Gina said as soon as Jody had joined them. She pointed, and Jody squinted. Four dorsal fins rose and fell through the surface of the glittering water, before all four dolphins leapt into the air in perfect synchronicity.

'Bottlenoses again,' said Jody immediately, her heart lifting as it always did. 'I think I saw that humpbacked dolphin again earlier,' she added. 'The one I saw at the beach – Dawn.'

'Are you sure?' said Gina, frowning. 'Brice did say they were a pretty rare sighting. It's a bit unlikely that you'd see the same one twice in one day, don't you think?'

Jody felt disappointed that her mother thought it was unlikely. She really wanted her parents to see the wonderful creature. The only person who had seen Dawn apart from Jody was Brice. It felt very strange, being the only one in her family who knew what Dawn looked like.

She walked back across the deck to see if the dugong was still there. But the seagrass meadow was still and quiet. The dugong had moved on. Jody took the opportunity of taking out her diary for a moment.

March 15 – afternoon – sitting on the deck of Kookaburra.

I felt pretty stupid just now. I honestly thought someone had fallen overboard on the Kookaburra *tour. I could see this figure sitting on the seabed, and I couldn't see any scuba equipment. I wondered if they'd got themselves tangled in the seagrass or something, and couldn't come up to breathe. It's true that I didn't exactly hear or see anyone fall overboard. But it looked so real So I yelled the place down. Well, what would you have done?*

I'm sure Dawn was following the Kookaburra I know Mom thought I was imagining things, but I felt her there. I don't know how else to explain it. I know I think about dolphins a lot, but I'm pretty sure I don't imagine them.

The squawk of an unfamiliar bird made Jody look up from the page. The *Kookaburra* moved closer into the shore of Fraser Island, where they could have a swim. The breakers along the shore were gentle and lazy – one of the benefits of a shoreline which faced mainland Australia and not the endless Pacific Ocean.

Jimmy and Sean wasted no time in stripping down to their trunks and leaping into the inviting water. Craig and Gina joined them, and one by one, most of the other *Kookaburra* passengers lowered themselves overboard as well. Jody put away her diary and sat at the prow of the boat, swinging her legs and deciding whether or not to go in. Part of her wanted to stay on the boat and keep watch on the horizon, in case Dawn returned. But the rest of her knew that the water would be lovely and cool.

'Come on, Brittany – let's go for a swim.'

Jody looked around to see Jason trying to coax Brittany over the side of the boat.

'Oh no.' Brittany shook her head vigorously. 'I'm not going in there. I'm staying right here, OK?'

Jason shrugged. 'Suit yourself.' He jumped overboard into the clear blue waves, one knee curled up underneath him for maximum splash. Then he struck off towards the twins, who were playing tag.

Jody thought it looked like fun, and prepared to jump in as well. 'You normally love swimming,' she said to Brittany curiously. 'Don't you want to come in?'

Brittany rolled her eyes. 'Don't you know anything, Jody?' she said fussily. 'Seawater is the worst thing for your hair. If it goes frizzy today, I'll just die.' She took off her sunhat and smoothed down her hair. 'I'm going inside for a bit, to check out this glass bottom you were raving about earlier,' she said. 'Hope it's as good as you said it was.'

Jody plunged down into the inviting water and swam over towards Sean, Jimmy and Jason. Within minutes, she was breathless and laughing, shaking water from her ears and eyes and trying to hold on to her slippery little brothers as they raced past.

Soon the boys were tired, and they all began to make their way back to the *Kookaburra*. The adults were already back on board, talking and laughing in the afternoon sunshine.

Jason paddled up to Jody. 'It's a shame Brittany didn't want to come in,' he said. 'She's kind of fun. You're not sisters, are you?'

Jody shook her head, and explained how Brittany had come to join their expedition.

'Tough call,' said Jason sympathetically. He looked back at the boat.

Jody knew he was wondering why Brittany hadn't come swimming. She couldn't tell him about Brittany's hair, because she knew Brittany would be mad.

'Brittany's quite a hard person to understand sometimes,' she said in the end. 'She said she wanted to check out the glass bottom of the boat, but I think she just wanted to be on her own for a while, you know?'

Suddenly Jason's eyes brightened. 'Hey! I've just had a great idea!' he said, beckoning Jody over. 'Listen to this! Brittany's going to love it.'

He whispered something in Jody's ear.

'You're not serious!' Jody cried.

'Are you on for it or not?' Jason insisted.

Jody shook her head firmly. Then she opened her mouth. 'Yes,' she found herself saying, to her astonishment. 'Why not?'

Jason grinned. 'Follow me.'

Jody swam after Jason as he quietly approached the side of the *Kookaburra*. They climbed aboard for a moment to get their breath back – then Jason turned, smiling, to Jody. 'Are you ready?' he asked.

Jody nodded. 'On the count of three,' she said. 'One, two, three, GO!'

She and Jason jumped back into the water. Then Jody took a deep breath and sank down under the water. She followed Jason back round towards the hull of the *Kookaburra*. With a swift kick of her legs, she ducked right underneath the hull – and swam beneath the glass bottom of the boat. A few moments later she popped up again, and took a huge gasping breath. Jason popped up beside her.

'Did you see her?' he asked eagerly.

Jody shook her head. 'I was too busy trying to get to the other side! What about you?'

'Well–' Jason began.

On the count of three . . .

Suddenly Jody could hear someone screaming on board the *Kookaburra*.

She looked across at Jason. 'I guess Brittany saw us,' she said, with a sinking feeling.

They both swam quietly up to the boat and scrambled up the ladder on to the deck. Jody could hear her mother's voice deep inside the cabin.

'Of course it wasn't a mermaid, sweetheart,' Gina was saying. 'You heard what Brice was saying about the sailors getting mistaken. It must have been a dugong.'

'It had hair!' Brittany was wailing. 'Long dark hair that waved behind it like seaweed! It wasn't a dugong Aunt Gina – honest!'

'Did it have a fish tail?' Sean's voice asked with interest.

Jody tugged on Jason's arm with a sigh. 'Come on,' she said. 'We'd better go explain. But I warn you. It's not going to be pretty.'

It was time to head back to Ocean's Point. Brittany had disappeared up to the cockpit with Brice and was refusing to come down, even though Jody and Jason had both apologized over and over again. Jason was sitting glumly at the prow of the boat, and Jimmy and Sean were running around the deck doing impressions of Brittany, screeching, 'It's a mermaid! It's a mermaid!'

Jody felt really bad about it. If there was one thing Brittany hated more than looking stupid, it was looking stupid in front of a boy.

'You've really done it this time, young lady,' Gina said severely.

Jody pulled a face. 'I know. I'm sorry,' she said. 'I didn't think Brittany would mistake me for a mermaid – I just thought it would be funny to wave at her when we swam under the boat. But I guess I forgot the waving part.'

Gina looked up at the cockpit. 'I suppose she'll get over it,' she said with a sigh. 'Eventually.'

Brice's voice floated down from the cockpit. 'In case you are interested after our rather exciting afternoon, I have a little treat for you as we leave Fraser Island today. If you look to your left, you'll see a couple of friendly faces.'

Jody looked – and gasped. The round, bronze-coloured head of a dugong was poking up above the water level, flaring its wide nostrils and snorting gently at the air. Beside the dugong was the smaller head of a calf, doing the same as its mother. Jody couldn't quite believe her eyes, but it looked as if the mother dugong was cradling the calf between her flippers, just like a human mother with a child.

'Your eyes aren't deceiving you,' Brice said through the loudspeaker. 'Dugongs do sit upright and hold their calves with their flippers, allowing the youngsters to suckle just like a human child would. We are very honoured to see one of the most loving sights in the animal kingdom. Let's do what we can to preserve these wonderful creatures. Now – time to head for home.'

March 15 – evening – back on the jetty at Ocean's Point after supper (fresh sausages!). I don't know what came over me earlier today. It was pretty funny, but it kind of backfired. Brittany is refusing to speak to me, and is in with her dad right now, asking to be moved to a different cabin. Unless she wants to sleep on deck, there's nowhere else for her to go, so I guess I'm just going to suffer the silent treatment tonight – and maybe for the next few days too. Jason's gutted. B told him that she never wants to speak to him again either. Mom told us off, but I think she saw the funny side. I feel bad for giving B such a fright, but we honestly didn't mean to. I should know by now that she's not very good at taking a joke!

Jody put down her diary and stretched out her legs in the cool evening air. Broken reflections of the low moon danced on the water, and she felt really lucky to be discovering more and more of the fascinating wildlife beneath the waves.

6

March 16 – after lunch – Ocean's Point harbour.

It's so beautiful and peaceful here. We've just been lazing around on the beach and checking out the harbour front cafés today. Maddie, Cam and Mei Lin thought the Kookaburra tour sounded so great that they've headed off to do it this afternoon. Mom, Dad, the twins and I are at the café now, where we've just had a fantastic lunch of fresh grilled fish. Dad and the boys just shared a huge ice-cream sundae that was almost as big as Jimmy and Sean put together!

Because Brittany's still pretty mad, she's done the opposite to us all morning. So when we were at the *beach, she was at the café, and the other way around. She's back on board* Dolphin Dreamer *now. She's wearing big dark glasses in case she sees Jason – I don't think she wants him to recognize her.*

The coastline stretches up to a small headland a little way south of here. I wonder what's on the other side? I might ask Dad if we can do some exploring this afternoon. Harry's been adjusting the tension on Dolphin Dreamer's *sails, and I think he'd like to try them out. Also there's been no sign of Dawn this morning. Maybe she's moved on down the coast?*

Jody closed her diary thoughtfully, and took another sip of her vanilla milkshake. If Dawn had moved further down the coast, maybe they wouldn't see her again. The thought upset her. She'd only seen Dawn for a few brief moments, but she knew there was something very special about her. Plus, she knew her parents would love to see the humpback dolphin. It would be such a shame if they never did.

Craig pushed back his chair. 'Well,' he said, 'I don't know about you guys, but I'm full to bursting here. That sundae finished me off.'

Gina laughed. 'You didn't have to have to have it, Craig,' she teased.

Craig shrugged with a twinkle in his eye. 'I know. But I'm on holiday!' he said.

Jody looked towards *Dolphin Dreamer*, which was bobbing quietly at its mooring.

'Dad,' she said. 'Do you think we could take *Dolphin Dreamer* down the coast today?'

'Cool!' said Jimmy and Sean together.

Craig took off his sunglasses and polished them on the hem of his shirt. 'I don't see why not,' he said after a moment. 'If Harry's up to it, it might be nice to do some exploring. I know Cam's with the *Kookaburra* this afternoon, but we can all lend Harry a hand. Let's talk to him when we get back to the boat, shall we?'

'What are we going to do about Brittany?' said Gina. 'We ought to ask her to come along as well.'

Jody frowned. She hadn't really thought about that. She knew their argument would blow over eventually, but Brittany was so unpredictable.

Jimmy and Sean groaned and rolled back in their chairs.

'She'll just complain all the time if she comes,' said Jimmy.

'Can't we leave her here?' Sean added.

Gina stood up from the café table. 'No,' she said in a decided voice. 'She's had all morning to herself, and I think it's time that she talked to us. We'll ask her very nicely, and Jody will apologize again. Then we can get back to normal.'

Jody opened her mouth to say that she didn't think Brittany would listen. But Gina held up her hand.

'I know you've apologized several times already, Jody,' she said gently. 'But Brittany will have to give in eventually. Why don't you buy her something from the shops here, and take it back to the boat? As a peace offering?'

Jody looked along the harbour front. There was one shop which sold trinkets and souvenirs. She might be able to find something.

'OK,' she agreed. She still had about five Australian dollars left over from the money her dad had given her that morning.

Gina looked relieved. 'Good girl,' she said. 'It's time we got this holiday back on a friendly footing.

We'll head back to the boat and discuss the idea of a short trip with Harry, OK?'

Jody wandered along the harbour front when her family had gone. There wasn't much in the souvenir shop. Ocean's Point was definitely a nature reserve, not a holiday resort. Giving up after about twenty minutes, she wandered down to the beach. She walked along the shore, kicking the little breakers which bubbled gently over her feet. What could she get for Brittany?

'Jody?' It was Jason, looking a little anxious and slightly out of breath. 'I saw you from over there,' he said, pointing towards the trees.

'Hi Jason,' Jody smiled.

Jason shuffled his feet in the sand. 'Is Brittany OK?'

Jody pulled a face. 'She's still in a bad mood,' she said. 'We all want to go on a coast cruise in *Dolphin Dreamer* this afternoon, but we have to cheer her up first. Got any ideas for a good present?' she added hopefully.

Jason grinned. He rummaged in his knapsack, which he had slung over his shoulder. 'I was hoping to see you today,' he said from the depths of his bag. 'Would you give Brittany this?'

He held out a magnificent shell. 'It's a nautilus,' he explained. 'I found it this morning. I'd like Brittany to have it. To say sorry.'

Jody stared at the shell. It was mottled pink and white, with a wonderful curling shape and a smooth mother-of-pearl interior. She held it up to her ear, and heard the whooshing sound of the sea.

'Jason, it's beautiful!' she exclaimed. 'Brittany will love it. You've saved my life!'

Jason shrugged. 'No worries,' he said shyly. He hefted his bag up over his shoulder again. 'See you around.'

Jody watched as Jason loped back up the beach and disappeared among the trees. Then she started running back to the harbour, clutching the precious shell.

Clattering down the jetty to reach *Dolphin Dreamer*, she saw her mother waiting for her.

'How did you get on?' asked Gina.

Jody grinned and waved the shell. 'Pretty good!'

With one leap, she jumped deftly aboard the boat and ran down the steps to the cabin she shared with

Brittany. Before her courage failed, she knocked on the door.

After a moment, the door opened a couple of centimetres.

'What do you want?' said Brittany sourly.

Jody leant against the door of the cabin and caught her breath. 'I saw Jason today,' she said.

Brittany blushed angrily. 'So?'

Jody held out the nautilus. 'He wanted me to give you this, and to tell you how sorry he is that he upset you. I'm sorry too.'

Brittany opened the door a little wider. She slowly took the shell, and turned it over in her hands. 'Does it sound like the sea when you listen to it?' she said at last.

'Yes!' said Jody, relieved. 'It's amazing. Try it!'

Brittany listened. A smile twitched at her lips. 'That's pretty cool,' she admitted.

Jody held her breath. Was she forgiven?

'I really am sorry, Brittany,' she repeated. 'Can we be friends again?'

Brittany weighed the shell in her hands, turning it around so that the light caught the beautiful mother of pearl shine. 'OK,' she said.

March 16 – afternoon – on the move!

Harry found this place called Golden Sands on the map, just south of the headland we can see. He rang the harbour master just now, so they are expecting us. It sounds like a fun place. I think it's more developed than Ocean's Point, with a bigger beach and more things to do. Jimmy and Sean think there'll be slot machines, and Brittany can't wait to see the shops. We left a message with the harbour master for Cam, Maddie and Mei Lin, telling them that we'd be back by supper time. Dr Taylor's come with us, but I don't think he approves of this new 'holiday jaunt', as he calls it.

Jody stretched her arms up high, feeling the rush of cool air against her skin. It was fun to be sailing again. Harry was keeping *Dolphin Dreamer* fairly close to the shore, so the water was still shallow and clear enough to see shoals of fish chasing each other across the seabed.

The long low flank of Fraser Island was still visible to the left as they slowly rounded the headland. *Dolphin Dreamer*'s hull shuddered against the buffeting of the changing currents, crashing through the waves and tilting with the wind.

At last the resort of Golden Sands came into view.

'Look!' Brittany pointed eagerly at the forest of masts and sails in the Golden Sands harbour.

When they'd arrived at Ocean's Point after four weeks at sea, it had felt like the busiest place on earth. But as they neared Golden Sands, Jody realized that it was nothing compared to the bustle of a real holiday resort. The Golden Sands sea front seemed to sprawl for over a mile, with brightly coloured shops, restaurants and arcades the whole way along. The beach sloped straight down from the seafront with the harbour tucked in the middle, neatly dividing the beach in two. As *Dolphin Dreamer* turned into the harbour, the smell of frying fish and spun sugar floated in the air and Jody could hear the unmistakable beat of loud holiday music. She felt very out of place suddenly, staring around at the busy scene. An image of Ocean's Point came into her mind. Oh, why had she suggested coming here? She knew immediately that she hated it.

Brittany's eyes were bright. 'This looks great!' she enthused, as Harry steered *Dolphin Dreamer* into a mooring with the help of Craig, who had jumped on to the pontoon to catch the ropes.

'This looks ghastly,' complained Dr Taylor, shading his eyes and wrinkling his nose in disgust. 'I have no idea what your parents were thinking of, agreeing to come to a place like this, Jody. It's so . . .' He searched for the word. 'Brash,' he finally declared.

'Well, life is all about contrasts, Dr Taylor,' said Gina, with a small frown on her face. 'I admit it's not really my kind of place either, but we're here now. So I think we should make the best of it, don't you?' She shouldered a beach bag and stepped down on to the pontoon. 'We'll only be here for a couple of hours. And you may find more leaflets to add to your dossier.'

'I don't think that anything here would provide appropriate material for my research,' fussed Dr Taylor. 'I shall simply stay on board and catch up on my latest correspondence with PetroCo.' He glanced at the seafront again and shuddered. 'Brash,' he muttered again, before disappearing below deck.

'Here is some money for everyone to spend as they please,' said Craig, handing Jody and the twins five dollars each. 'But that's your lot,' he cautioned. 'I'm not handing out any more, is that clear?'

'We're going to the slot machines,' said Sean and Jimmy immediately.

Harry pressed ten dollars into Brittany's hand. 'I know that you miss the lively life sometimes, Brittany,' he said apologetically. 'So now's your chance to enjoy yourself.'

'I want some new sunglasses,' Brittany decided. '*If* I can find any for only ten dollars,' she added pointedly.

'Well,' said Harry after a moment, 'a challenge like that is always more fun. Don't you think?'

Brittany scowled, but she tucked the money carefully into her pocket anyway.

The smell of frying and burnt sugar was much stronger now that they were ashore. There seemed to be hundreds of people browsing along the seafront, all eating dripping ice creams and chips from greasy bags. Jody found that most of them seemed to be walking towards her, and she had to push her way through the oncoming crowd. A soggy crisp bag suddenly blew up and into her face, giving her a fright. Her parents seemed miles ahead.

Jody felt a pang for the peace and quiet of Ocean's Point. She'd known straight away that Golden Sands wasn't her kind of place, but there was something else about the resort that was making her uneasy.

She saw litter blowing in the wind, swirling along the boardwalk and down on to the shoreline. People were crowded together on the beach, and the sea had a strange, oily sheen of sun cream floating on its surface.

'There you are!' Gina exclaimed when Jody finally caught up with her family. 'We thought we'd lost you.'

Craig looked worried. 'It's going to be very easy to get lost here,' he said. 'I any of you do get lost, you must promise me now that you'll make your way back to *Dolphin Dreamer*.'

Brittany rolled her eyes. 'I'm not totally stupid, you know,' she said.

Jimmy and Sean promised faithfully not to get lost, and then charged into the nearest arcade.

'I'll go with the boys,' said Craig, checking his watch. 'Shall we meet back at the boat around four o'clock?'

Jody looked along the shoreline. Several hundred metres away, the crowds seemed to thin out a little. 'I'm going to walk along the beach,' she said.

'Getting away from the crowds?' Gina guessed.

Jody laughed. Her mother knew her pretty well.

Brittany shook her head. 'I don't get you, Jody,'

she said. 'We've got peace and quiet at Ocean's Point. We wanted something different today, so we came to Golden Sands. Look at all these shops! I'm going to look for sunglasses. Coming, Aunt Gina?'

Jody waved goodbye, and made her way down to the waterfront. She had to walk for almost fifteen minutes before she found a quieter, more secluded part of the beach. It was unlikely that she'd see any marine life. There were simply too many people around. Still, she decided it was better than all the jostling around the harbour.

Suddenly she realized what was making her uneasy. She hadn't seen a single warden or lifeguard along the beaches or by the harbour. At Ocean's Point, the wardens were easily recognized in their green polo shirts. She knew that Golden Sands wasn't a nature reserve, but Brice had made it sound as if the whole of the Queensland coastline was special and needed looking after. Golden Sands felt like a place that didn't know about its responsibility for the sea and the beaches. Her sense of unease grew stronger.

She began to wade out into the water. About a hundred metres out, she was still only up to her thighs. The shallows stretched out for another half a mile before the colour of the water grew deeper and bluer.

Some distance to her left, she noticed a group of people standing together in the waves. They seemed to be looking at something. Shading her eyes from the sun, she stared.

It was a dolphin. Jody could hardly believe her eyes. A wild dolphin, in water as shallow as this? Wading quickly towards the crowd, she realized something else The people were reaching out to the dolphin and touching it. Worse still, they were *feeding* it.

'Stop!' she called. 'You shouldn't feed the dolphins, please stop!'

The crowd was too far away to hear her, or they were just ignoring her. Jody tried to wade quicker, but the water sucked at her legs, slowing her down.

A sharp whistle behind her made her stop in her tracks. Turning around, she came face to face with a pink and white-coloured dolphin, whose hump and colour-splashed beak made her heart leap in her chest.

'Dawn!' she whispered. 'Is that you?'

You mustn't feed the dolphins!

The humpbacked dolphin approached her. With a shiver, Jody stared into the depths of one wild, bright eye. She was sure it was Dawn! The dolphin clicked gently, and nodded her beak in the air.

She wants food, Jody realized. 'I don't have anything for you,' she said quietly, trying not to remember all the terrible things Brice had told her about dolphins who became dependent on handouts. 'You shouldn't be asking for food, Dawn! It's not good for you.'

She waved her hands at the dolphin as gently as she could. She didn't want to scare her, but she had to send her back out to sea.

Dawn rolled over and dived. For one brief moment, Jody thought she had succeeded. Then she saw Dawn resurface – right next to the group of tourists Jody had been trying to approach.

With a dull feeling of inevitability, Jody watched one of the tourists reach out towards Dawn, offering her one of his chips. A burst of laughter floated across the water.

'Don't you realize what you're doing?' Jody called across the water. 'It's wrong to feed dolphins!'

One of the tourists turned and stared at her. He

was young, with sunburned shoulders and a stripe of pink sunblock across his nose.

'But it's hungry,' he called back. 'We're not doing any harm. Why don't you go and bother someone else?'

Jody realized that it was pointless trying to talk to them. She turned around and waded back to shore as fast as she could. She had to tell someone. She had to stop this – before something terrible happened!

7

'Jody, what on earth has happened?' exclaimed Harry when Jody rushed aboard. 'Are you all right?'

'Harry, they're feeding the dolphins!' Jody cried. Her chest hurt from running up the beach, and she'd stumbled and banged her elbow on one of the seafront lampposts. Craig and the twins had moved to another arcade, and she hadn't been able to see Gina or Brittany through the sea of shoppers, so she had run straight back to *Dolphin Dreamer*.

Harry looked confused. 'Who's feeding the dolphins?'

'Tourists.' Jody leant against the mast, catching her breath. 'They were feeding them chips, and oh, Harry! I saw Dawn the humpbacked dolphin again. They were feeding her too!'

Dr Taylor poked his head out of the cabin. 'What's all the racket?' he asked.

Jody related her story again.

Dr Taylor heaved a deep and knowing sigh. 'What did I tell you?' he said, shaking his head. 'This is a terrible place. The sooner we get out of here, the better.'

'No, Dr Taylor!' cried Jody. 'Leaving's the last thing we should do! We have to help the dolphins. We have to tell someone.'

Harry scratched his head. 'Did you see any wardens?' he asked at last. 'They'd be the ones to tell, I suppose.'

Jody shook her head. 'I don't think that there are any in Golden Sands,' she said. 'That's half the problem.'

Harry looked along the pontoon at the sound of approaching feet. 'Here comes your mom,' he said, pointing. 'She'll know what to do.' He patted Jody kindly on the shoulder, and disappeared to the stern of the ship.

Jody had never been so glad to see anyone in her life as Gina and Brittany made their way towards them.

'Mom, come quickly!' she called. 'I have to talk to you!'

'Hi to you too, Jody,' said Brittany, sounding a bit put out.

'Sorry Brittany, but this is an emergency,' Jody apologized.

Dr Taylor raised his hands. 'I've heard the story already and offered my opinion,' he said gravely. 'Now I shall leave the solution to the experts.'

Jody recounted what she'd seen as fast and as clearly as she could. By the time she'd finished, Gina's face was pale with shock.

'Feeding dolphins *chips*?' she repeated, as if she could hardly believe her ears.

'Gross,' Brittany said, flipping her new lilac-coloured sunglasses up into her hair.

'The dolphins will be OK, won't they?' Jody asked anxiously.

Gina sighed and shook her head. 'You know the dangers of feeding wild dolphins, Jody. Anything could happen. Apart from an increasing dependency on food handouts from tourists, the dolphins are open to all kinds of problems. Poisoning, the spread of contagious diseases, obesity – they are all very real dangers. Where on earth were the wardens?'

'It's not a marine reserve like Ocean's Point,' Jody pointed out unhappily. 'I don't think they have wardens. I didn't see any. I didn't even see any lifeguards.'

Gina shook her head. 'You don't have to be a marine reserve to take responsibility for your immediate environment. There's no excuse for allowing this kind of unchecked behaviour. The Pacific is home to so many wild creatures – it's a crime to allow them to be exploited in this way.'

Jody's eyes filled with tears. 'What are we going to do? We have to stop the tourists from feeding the dolphins!'

'What's up?' Craig appeared on the deck with the twins, who promptly raced down the cabin steps to play with their new pack of Golden Sands playing cards.

Jody was halfway through the story for the fourth time when there was a loud splash off the bow.

'What was that?' Gina asked with surprise.

Jody rushed to the edge of the boat, her fears suddenly forgotten. She had the strangest feeling in her stomach. Could it be . . . ?

'Mom, Dad, come quick!' she called. She didn't care how odd she sounded. 'I think it's Dawn!'

'You can't possibly know that,' scoffed Brittany. 'You only heard a splash!'

Jody couldn't explain the strange feeling that had come over her. 'Trust me. I looked into Dawn's eyes earlier. She's come to find me.'

'Dawn, the humpbacked dolphin you saw yesterday?' said Craig in astonishment. 'Here?'

'I didn't get to that part, Dad,' said Jody, leaning over the railing and looking up and down the harbour. 'Dawn was here. She obviously swam down the coast, like Brice thought. The tourists were feeding her too.'

A fin rose and fell in the water at the mouth of the harbour. Suddenly the surface of the water broke, and a dolphin arced up into the air.

'What unusual colouring,' remarked Gina, shading her eyes. 'And I can see the hump!'

At last, Jody's parents had seen her mystery dolphin.

Breaking the waves

'I knew it!' Jody said, delighted that Dawn had come to find her. 'Look, she's leaping again!'

Jody watched happily as Dawn flung herself out of the water. She'd almost forgotten about the worrying incident at the beach – this was such a beautiful sight.

'She's not leaping very high,' observed Craig, frowning.

Jody thought about it. Her father was right. When she had first seen Dawn at Ocean's Point, the dolphin had made a much higher leap. Now her tail was barely leaving the surface of the water before she fell back down again.

The feeling of unease Jody had felt on the beach came surging back. Suddenly she felt sick.

Dawn swam in circles at the mouth of the harbour, expelling air hard and fast from her blowhole.

'It looks like she's having breathing difficulties,' said Gina, leaning over the boat for a better look.

'Brice said that she was looking a bit overweight,' said Craig. 'That's probably having an effect.'

With one lazy flick of her tail, Dawn disappeared beneath the water. Jody watched as the dolphin left a rippling wake behind her, and swam out to sea.

'Something's wrong with her,' Jody said slowly.

'I'm sure she's fine,' said Brittany.

Suddenly Jody felt as if she was calling to the tourists again and being ignored. She swung around to Brittany. 'Something's wrong with that dolphin!' she shouted. 'Why don't you care? Golden Sands is dirty and dangerous. I wish we'd never come!' she added passionately.

'Well, now,' said a strange voice. 'Never is a pretty strong word.'

Startled, Jody looked across the water to the

neighbouring boat. The owner of the voice was sitting on the deck of a gleaming white pleasure cruiser, staring at her with interest.

'I said, never is a pretty strong word,' he repeated, picking up a tumbler from a small table and standing up. He gestured at Jody with his drink. 'What's got you so worked up, young lady?' he asked. 'It's a beautiful day, and we're in a beautiful place. Golden Sands has nothing but happy vibes.'

'Happy vibes?' Jody repeated. 'What do you mean?'

The stranger laughed. 'Just look around you! This place is all about pleasure and relaxation. The tourists are happy, the money rolls in. That's what life's about, in my book.'

'Mine too,' said Brittany, staring with interest at the stranger's boat.

Jody noticed the boat's name, *Big Boy*, printed in bold red letters across the bow. Then she looked up at the seafront. All she could see was crowds and dirt, and the painful memory of Dawn taking chips from an ignorant tourist. She felt her temper rising. 'People were feeding dolphins out there,' she said. 'They shouldn't do that.'

'Hey, cool down,' said the stranger, taking a long

gulp from his tumbler. 'I love dolphins. They're beautiful creatures. But they can't always find food in the ocean, so they make the best of what they can find. It's all a question of survival.'

'My wife and I are marine biologists,' said Craig, 'and I can tell you this for a fact, sir. If dolphins become too dependent on handouts, not only do the dolphins themselves suffer, but a delicate ecological balance is lost. The cost is too terrible to consider.'

The stranger shook his head, with a smile playing about his lips. 'I suggest you quit worrying so much. You're on holiday, I take it? So enjoy!'

With another languid wave of his hand, he sauntered inside the cabin of *Big Boy*.

'He doesn't seem to care!' Jody said in surprise, watching him disappear from sight. The idea that someone might not be interested in the fate of a group of wild dolphins filled her with horror.

Gina shook her head. 'It seems not,' she said in a resigned voice. 'Come on. I think we've all had enough of Golden Sands, don't you? I suggest we get back to Ocean's Point straight away, and report everything we've seen to Brice. If this place doesn't have wardens, you can bet your life that Brice will want to do something about it.'

Jody stayed up on deck as *Dolphin Dreamer* left Golden Sands and headed for the open sea again. She needed to feel the cool, salty air on her skin, to wash away the dirt and the memories of Golden Sands. Her mind kept returning to the man on board *Big Boy*. She couldn't understand why he had been like that – so uninterested in the dolphins. He had a boat, so he obviously knew how to sail. Didn't the sea and all its natural wonders interest him at *all*?

'What do you think of my sunglasses, Jody?' Brittany appeared beside her, striking a model pose with her glasses balanced on the end of her nose. 'Cool, aren't they? And they were only eight dollars.'

'They're nice,' said Jody absently.

'Nice?' Brittany echoed. 'Is that the best you can do?'

Jody sighed. 'Sorry. I'm just thinking about something else.'

'No prizes for guessing what,' said Brittany. 'Don't worry about the dolphins,' she said unexpectedly.

'Brice will know what to do. He'll be able to help them.'

Brittany was full of surprises, Jody thought. One minute she's a prima donna, and the next she comes out with something unexpectedly kind and thoughtful. Maybe the McGraths' love of dolphins was rubbing off on her after all.

Dolphin Dreamer rounded the headland again, and Jody watched Ocean's Point come into view. In a funny way, it felt like coming home. It was strange how attached she had become to the place, even though they'd only been there for a couple of days.

Brice was talking to the harbour master when they arrived. Maddie, Cam and Mei Lin were sitting in a row on the pontoon and dangling their legs in the water.

'Had a good time?' Cam called, jumping to his feet to catch the rope Harry threw at him.

'Not exactly,' said Craig. 'Brice, we need a word with you. Have you got a moment?'

Brice checked his watch. 'Sure,' he said easily. 'Come on down to *Kookaburra* while I tidy up. We can talk there.'

'Can I come, Dad?' Jody asked.

'Of course,' said Craig. 'After all, you witnessed the problem. Come on.'

'So, what's this about?' Brice asked, as Jody and her parents walked beside him along the battered old boardwalk, towards the *Kookaburra*.

'We've just been to Golden Sands,' said Jody.

Brice nodded slowly. 'I think I can guess what you are about to say.'

'You can?' Jody was surprised.

'We know about the resorts south of here,' said Brice, jumping neatly aboard the *Kookaburra* and offering the others a hand. 'Dirty and overcrowded, right?'

'More than that,' said Gina grimly.

Brice was silent as Jody told him what she'd seen.

'Well,' he said at last. 'I knew it was bad, but not that bad. You actually saw people feeding dolphins?'

'They were feeding a dolphin chips!' said Jody. She still found it hard to believe. 'And it wasn't just any dolphin, Brice. It was Dawn. Remember you said that she was looking overweight? You were right about her scavenging around other resorts.'

'We saw her in the harbour,' added Craig. 'She seemed to be having breathing difficulties.'

Brice nodded. 'That would probably be down to the extra weight,' he said. 'Listen, I know the owner of Golden Sands. His name is Bob Andrews. He's not a bad guy, just the kind of guy who enjoys the easy life. He probably doesn't know the half of what goes on. Why don't we pay him a visit tomorrow morning? Golden Sands is only forty minutes by road. It may be worth talking to him now that Jody has seen the situation with her own eyes. And since you guys are respected marine biologists, you'll have plenty of facts about the dangers of dolphin dependency and unregulated human contact. What do you say?'

'Let's do it,' said Craig immediately. 'This needs to be cleared up before any more damage is done. And when I meet Mr Andrews, I'm going to give him a piece of my mind!'

8

March 16 – evening – on the beach at Ocean's Point.
Dad is swimming with Sean and Jimmy in the sunset
as I'm writing this. I know I've said that Ocean's Point
is beautiful, but after Golden Sands it's somehow magical
as well. All I can hear is the splashing of the waves
(and of Dad and the boys!) and the noisy flapping of
birds' wings as they all come home to roost in the trees
behind me. But even though it's magical, I'm restless. I
want to go to Golden Sands NOW and talk to Mr Andrews
about the dolphins. I probably won't get any sleep
tonight – I'll be too busy worrying about Dawn. Is she
OK? I wish it was morning already...

*   *   *

'Time to go, Jody.'

Jody groaned and opened her eyes. Her mother was smiling at her.

'It's half past eight. Brice thought it would take about an hour to get to Golden Sands, and we want to go before the heat of the day kicks in.'

Jody quickly wriggled into a T-shirt and a pair of shorts, brushed her teeth and ran a comb through her dark hair. She walked into the galley and grabbed a bread roll and some honey, and came out on deck.

The morning was bright and cool, but the haze on the horizon suggested that it would be a hot day. Brice was waiting for them beside a battered red pick-up truck, dangling a set of keys.

'It's about thirty miles,' he explained as they set off, rumbling over the pits and ridges of the old Ocean's Point road. 'But it's a great route. The views along the coast are stunning. Enjoy!'

It felt strange doing the journey to Golden Sands by land this time. The coastline stretched behind and ahead of them, and the multi-coloured beaches and cliff gleamed in the early morning light. There were huge sand dunes all along the roadside, whipped into strange sculpted shapes by the wind and the sea.

About twenty minutes along the route, Jody was a huge bird dive down into the sea and emerge again with a large wriggling fish clutched in its powerful talons.

'Osprey,' Brice explained, expertly negotiating the odd drifts of sand which had swept across the road's surface. 'We have white-breasted sea eagles too, and peregrine falcons.'

The salty smell of Golden Sands blew through the open window as Brice swung into the car park. 'Follow me,' he said, beckoning them towards the harbour.

'Does Mr Andrews live on a boat?' asked Jody.

'He certainly does,' said Brice. 'It's quite a pleasure cruiser. Although to be honest, he doesn't take it out to sea very often. I think he likes the sound of the waves, but he prefers the bustle of the resort.' He pointed down the pontoon to a boat moored near the mouth of the harbour. 'That's his boat there.'

Jody gasped. Brice was pointing at *Big Boy*. The owner of Golden Sands, Bob Andrews, was none other than yesterday's stranger!

'Brice—' she started to say.

But Brice was striding down the pontoon towards *Big Boy*, and it was too late to explain.

'This should be interesting,' remarked Craig.

'He didn't listen to us yesterday,' said Jody anxiously, as they followed Brice towards *Big Boy*. 'Why should be listen today?'

'We didn't introduce ourselves yesterday,' Gina reminded her. 'Perhaps when we've explained what we do, and we've had a chance to put the actual facts to him, he'll listen to us.'

Jody hoped with all her heart that her mother was right. But deep down, she had a nasty feeling that it would make no difference if they introduced themselves or not. Mr Andrews would never care, and that was that.

Brice and Bob Andrews were waiting for them on the deck of *Big Boy*.

'Hello again,' said Bob Andrews smoothly when Brice made the introductions.

Brice looked confused. 'You know each other?'

'We met yesterday,' said Craig, extending his hand. Bob Andrews shook it genially. 'We just didn't get as far as exchanging names.'

Bob Andrews waved Jody and her family aboard. 'Are we talking about dolphins again?' he asked.

'We are,' said Gina. 'We appreciate you meeting us, Mr Andrews. We don't want to disturb your morning any more than we have to.'

Bob Andrews offered them a seat in the luxurious, white leather interior of *Big Boy*. Jody noticed with interest that the boat had a glass floor like the *Kookaburra*.

Bob Andrews saw Jody staring. 'Like it?' he said. 'You can see all kinds of things through there.'

'I know,' said Jody politely. '*Kookaburra* has one at Ocean's Point.'

While Bob Andrews fixed drinks for everyone, Brice explained that *Kookaburra* was the Ocean's Point tour boat. 'We like to take tourists out into deeper water, to the coast of Fraser Island,' he said.

'Fraser Island, eh?' Bob Andrews handed around tea and coffee in gleaming glass and chrome cups. 'I've never been.'

Jody was astonished. He had a boat, and he'd never been to Fraser Island? What did Mr Andrews do with his time?

'The idea of the tour boat is to view dolphins and

whales away from the coast,' Brice said. 'That way, we hope to discourage dolphins from coming too close in to shore.'

'But where's the pleasure in that?' Bob Andrews objected. 'The great appeal of Golden Sands is that we keep things natural.' Bob Andrews was expanding on his theme. 'The ocean doesn't belong to anybody. Tourists want to see dolphins for free. They don't want to pay for boat trips.'

'Mr Andrews,' said Craig. 'I don't think you fully understand the consequences of encouraging unsupervised human interaction with dolphins.'

Bob Andrews smiled indulgently. 'I assure you, Dr McGrath, that as the owner of Golden Sands, I have never had any problem with the dolphins. The tourists love Golden Sands just the way it is. Why else would they return, year after year?' He stood up. 'It's been a pleasure talking to you, but I do have to be getting on with things. Would you excuse me? I'm sorry I couldn't be much help.'

It was impossible to continue the conversation without appearing rude. Jody stood up slowly, and followed her parents out on to the deck.

'I'm sorry you had a wasted trip,' Bob Andrews began.

'Sir!' came a breathless voice from the pontoon. 'Mr Andrews, sir!'

Jody saw a young man in a bright yellow T-shirt emblazoned with the logo *Golden Sands for a Golden Time*. He seemed agitated.

'Mr Andrews, sir!' he said again. He looked at Jody and her parents with an apologetic smile.

Bob Andrews looked irritated. 'What is it, Davis?'

'Dawson, sir,' said the young man. 'Sorry to interrupt.'

Bob Andrews raised his eyebrows. 'Well?'

'Someone's found a sick dolphin, sir,' said Dawson.

Jody clutched her mother's arm instinctively. A sick dolphin?

Craig stepped forward. 'How sick?' he said urgently.

Dawson looked surprised. He glanced across at his boss.

'This is Dr McGrath, a visiting zoologist,' said Bob Andrews.

Craig didn't bother to correct him. 'What are the

symptoms?' he asked, stepping down from *Big Boy* on to the pontoon.

'It's hard to tell, Dr McGrath,' said Dawson. 'I don't really know about dolphins. I just work at the information booth on the sea front. A tourist found it.'

Bob Andrews looked more alert. 'A tourist?' he repeated with a frown. 'That's not good.'

'It looks serious, sir,' said Dawson anxiously. 'It might even be catching.'

Bob Andrews jumped down on the ponton. 'Let's go,' he said.

Jody's heart leapt. It seemed that Bob Andrews did care, after all!

'If the other dolphins catch it, we may have a problem on our hands,' Bob Andrews said, striding up the pontoon. 'The reputation of Golden Sands will suffer.'

Jody hurried after him, followed closely by her parents. 'There's a sick dolphin out there!' she said anxiously. 'Can't you do anything?'

Bob Andrews looked faintly uncomfortable. 'You can't get too attached to dolphins, young lady,' he said. 'They are wild creatures, and—'

'They are indeed wild,' interrupted Gina grimly. 'And that is why human interaction should be discouraged.'

Bob Andrews opened his mouth, and then closed it again. After a pause, he said, 'Where is it, Dawson?'

'We've penned it into a shallow area on the north beach, sir,' replied the young man. They had now reached the seafront, where crowds of tourists were beginning to assemble.

Half-running, half-walking, Dawson led them to the north beach, the one Jody hadn't explored the previous day. Jody's head was bursting with questions and worries. What was the matter with the dolphin? Was it really as serious as Dawson thought?

At last, they reached the penned-in shallow area. Jody was shocked at the state of it. The nets looked old and mildewed, and the enclosure wasn't nearly as big as it should have been. A couple of tourists were sitting on the sand, chatting and keeping half an eye on the enclosure. Jody presumed they were the ones who had found the dolphin.

She approached more closely. The sick dolphin was lying motionless on the surface of the water, its

Dawn's very sick.

breathing fast and shallow. Jody almost cried out loud when she saw the distinctive hump below the sick animal's dorsal fin. Her worst nightmare had come true.

Brice recognized the dolphin immediately. 'It's Dawn,' he said quickly. 'You were right. Something is definitely wrong.'

Craig looked around. 'Where is the vet?' he asked Bob Andrews.

The owner of Golden Sands was biting at the nail on his little finger. Jody watched him. He was looking increasingly uncomfortable.

Dawson broke the silence. 'I don't think we have one, Dr McGrath.'

'You don't have a vet?' said Craig in disbelief. He waded over to the pen and gently placed his hand on Dawn's hump while he bent to listen to her breathing. Dawn rolled slightly in the water. Craig was checking the timing of Dawn's breaths against his watch. 'She's definitely breathing much too rapidly,' Craig said gravely. 'Something is seriously wrong.'

He beckoned to Gina. 'Come and listen,' he said. 'Her breathing is laboured and there's quite a strong smell to it. That's a sure sign of a respiratory infection.'

Craig and Gina conferred in quiet, serious voices for a few moments. Then Craig made a quick examination of the distressed dolphin, looking carefully at her blowhole where Jody could see some mucus oozing out. Just then, Dawn seemed to shudder and make a sneezing sound.

'Do you know what's wrong, Dad?' Jody asked in a wobbly voice. Brice put a comforting arm around her shoulders.

'I have an idea,' Craig said, and then stopped. 'No,' he corrected with a frown. 'It's not possible.'

'Try us,' encouraged Gina, her hand resting soothingly on Dawn's back.

Craig looked up. His face was puzzled. 'This is going to sound very strange,' he said, slowly shaking his head, 'but the closest thing I can come up with doesn't normally relate to dolphins at all.' He looked across at Jody. 'In fact, I'm going purely on something I remember about you, Jody.'

'Me?' Jody was confused.

Craig nodded. 'Do you remember when you were about eight? You got so sick that we had to take you to hospital for observation.'

Jody had a faint memory of long white corridors that smelt of pine floor cleaner, and a machine that bleeped by her bed.

'If you're thinking . . .' Gina began.

Craig held up his hand. 'I know it sounds crazy,' he said, 'but that's exactly what I'm thinking. It looks like Dawn could have a bad case of viral pneumonia. It's treatable in humans, but I've never heard of a case involving a dolphin.'

He turned to Bob Andrews and looked him

squarely in the eye. 'If I'm right about this, Mr Andrews, you have a very serious situation on your hands. It looks as though this animal has contracted a disease from humans. And there is a very grave danger that she will die.'

9

Jody had never seen anyone look as shocked as Bob Andrews did at that moment. His jaw fell open and his deeply tanned face turned a shade of grey.

'Die?' he repeated, as if he couldn't believe what he'd just heard. 'Just because it's been in contact with a few tourists?'

Craig waded back to the beach. 'We need to get this animal to a vet as quickly as we can. Brice, I suggest we take her back to Ocean's Point in the back of your truck.'

Jody stared at her dad. She knew that wherever

possible, dolphins were transported by water. It was too dangerous for them to be moved any other way, because their bodies needed the water's natural support. Their internal organs could be crushed, and their skin could dehydrate. It was a horrible responsibility.

Brice was clearly thinking the same thing. 'It's a forty-minute ride by road, and we're approaching the hottest part of the day,' he warned. 'We may do more harm than good if we put Dawn in the truck.'

'I know.' Craig looked grim. 'But I don't think we have any choice. It would take at least a couple of hours to move her by boat. That's too long, given the seriousness of her condition. This animal needs immediate treatment. It's a risk we have to take.'

Everyone looked at the sick dolphin, who was lying quietly in the netted enclosure. Her flanks were rising and falling rapidly as she struggled to catch her breath.

'I can stay in the back of the truck with Dawn,' said Jody impulsively. 'I'll sluice her with water the whole way. We can put up a shade to protect her from the sun.'

'We need equipment to move Dawn into the truck,' said Gina. 'And we need a sling to transport her properly.'

'I already thought of that,' said Brice. 'After everything you told me, I put a sling in the truck, just in case. I was hoping we wouldn't have to use it.'

'We still need a winch to lift her on to the truck,' said Gina anxiously.

'Perhaps I can help there.'

Jody turned around. In the seriousness of the situation, she had completely forgotten about Bob Andrews.

'We have a winch that we use in the harbour, for getting boats up and into dry dock for repairs,' said the owner of Golden Sands. 'Would that be any use?'

Craig thought about it. 'Is it mobile?' he said.

'As far as I know, yes.' Bob Andrews turned to Dawson and gave him a set of brief instructions.

As Dawson ran up the beach towards the harbour, Brice started running in the same direction. 'I'll fetch the truck,' he called back over his shoulder. 'I'll bring it right down on to the sand, as close as I can. Then I'll need some help constructing the sling.'

Jody waded into the water, and approached Dawn as slowly as she could. Making soothing, clicking sounds with her tongue, she leaned over the netting. 'We'll look after you,' she promised, trying to sound confident. 'You'll be fine once you get to Ocean's Point.'

She sluiced some sea water gently over Dawn's shivering back, taking care not to splash water across the dolphin's blowhole.

She felt her mother's hand on her shoulder.

'Jody, we need some water to go in the back of the truck,' said Gina. 'Can you arrange the buckets with Mr Andrews? He should have several on board his boat. You'll need to sluice Dawn regularly. Brice should have some kind of canopy for the truck, so we can at least shield her from the sun.'

Jody nodded, grateful that her mother was trusting her with such an important task. She reluctantly tore herself away from Dawn's side, and followed Bob Andrews up the beach towards *Big Boy*.

Bob Andrews didn't say a word as they approached the harbour. Jody was glad. She wasn't sure that she would be able to have a normal conversation with him after all that had happened.

She obediently took the stack of large, empty buckets he handed to her, and headed back down to the beach with them.

Halfway there, she looked back briefly. Bob Andrews was standing alone on the deck of *Big Boy*, watching. He raised his hand once, and then walked slowly back inside the cabin.

Jody soon forgot about him as she approached the others. Craig and Gina were busy constructing the sling, and Dawson had returned with the harbour master, who had driven the harbour winch down to the beach.

Brice looked up from the back of the truck, where he was trying to fix the cradle which would hold Dawn in her sling. 'Range the buckets either side of the cradle would you, Jody?' he said. 'We'll fill them with sea water in a minute.'

The buckets were filled with the help of an electric pump, and at last, the winch lowered the sling into the netted enclosure.

Dawn flinched briefly, but was too tired and unwell to put up any kind of fight. As Craig and Gina gently fitted the sling around her inert body, the winch took up the slack. Lifting Dawn cleanly out of the water, the Golden Sands harbour master manoeuvred the sling until it was directly over the cradle in the truck.

Brice gave the thumbs-up as the sling settled into place. Then he deftly drew up the cream-coloured roof canvas and fixed it into place, providing some welcome shade. Jody scrambled on to the truck, and took up her position beside Dawn.

'Ready to go!' cried Brice.

And they were off.

Dawn has to get to Ocean Point – and quick!

March 17 – afternoon – Ocean's Point.
I hope I never have to do anything like that road journey again. Dawn was as good as gold, even though it was a really bumpy ride. I think I got more water on me than on Dawn, because Brice was going really fast, and it's not a very smooth road – I've got bruises all over my legs and arms. I didn't see the coastal view or anything this time. I was just concentrating on Dawn as I sluiced her over and over again. I was really glad when the truck reached Ocean's Point, because I was down to my last bucket.

Brice's boss, David, is a qualified marine vet. Brice had radioed him so he knew we were coming. Brice drove straight down on to the beach and some way along until we reached a shallow inlet where David had a bag of medicine and a winch ready and waiting. Dawn is now safely in the water, but she isn't looking very good. We're taking it in turns to watch her, in case there's any change. Please PLEASE let Dawn be all right. I don't know what I'll do if she dies.

Jody clutched her diary as she hovered anxiously around the inlet, where her father and David Meers, the marine vet and chief warden of Ocean's

Point, were tending to the sick dolphin.

'Go back to the boat,' Craig told her. 'You'll need some rest if you're going to be on watch this evening.'

Jody pulled a face. 'Do I have to go back? I feel so useless there.'

David waded out of the water. He was a tall man with a shock of black hair and a deeply tanned face. He reminded Jody of someone, but she couldn't think who. 'Are you taking a watch later on, young lady?' he said to her.

Jody nodded. Of course she was. She'd offered to take the midnight watch, because she knew that Dawn would need her then. She remembered being ill, waking up in the middle of the night and not being able to get back to sleep. It was the loneliest time of all.

David smiled at her. 'Well, in that case you do need some rest,' he urged gently.

It was one thing to argue with her father, but quite another thing to argue with David. Meekly Jody left them to it, casting worried glances over her shoulder as she walked away down the beach.

She was nearly at the harbour when a face she recognized appeared beside her.

'Hey, Jody,' said Jason.

That's why David had looked familiar! Jody suddenly realized that he looked just like Jason. Tall, tanned – and with that unmistakable shock of black hair, which stood up even when it was soaked with seawater.

Jason saw her expression and laughed. 'I guess you've just met my dad.'

'How did you know?' Jody was surprised.

Jason shrugged. 'People get this expression on their face when they meet us both. It's like, "you two *must* be related".'

Jody grinned. 'You do look just like him,' she agreed. She was glad for a lighter moment to lift the tension she was feeling.

They walked the last few metres to the harbour together.

'So,' Jason said hesitantly. 'Do you think Brittany will speak to me now?'

Jody considered the question. 'She really liked the shell,' she said. 'I think it's worth a try.'

Jason smiled with relief. 'Will you tell her that I'll be on the beach for the rest of the afternoon?'

Jody agreed, and waved to him as she stepped

down on to the pontoon. *Dolphin Dreamer* was rocking gently in the current, looking cosy and homelike. Jody suddenly thought of her bed with longing. She was tired, she realized. It had been a long day.

Dr Taylor was sitting on the deck with a pair of binoculars trained on the ocean horizon. He looked around at Jody's approach.

'Ah Jody,' he said gravely. 'Any news on the dolphin?'

Jody hung her head and scuffed at the sand on the pontoon. 'It's the same as earlier, really. David's been with her since she arrived, but it's not looking very good.'

She knew that if she talked about Dawn any more, she would cry, so she changed the subject. 'Have you seen any interesting birds, Dr Taylor?'

'I'm watching the pelicans,' Dr Taylor explained, indicating his binoculars. 'A little break every now and again is important for the soul . . . when one is engaged in important research,' he added hurriedly.

Dr Taylor's forehead and nose were red and sunburned. It was clear that he'd been spending most of his time out in the open air at Ocean's Point, rather than down in his cabin with his books.

'They are quite extraordinary creatures, with their wonderful black and white plumage and their dark blue feet,' Dr Taylor continued with enthusiasm. 'Have you seen any since our arrival?'

Jody told him about the pelicans she'd seen at Fraser Island, as well as the diving osprey on the road to Golden Sands.

The sound of an approaching boat made her turn and look out to sea. A sleek red and white motorboat was making its way towards the harbour. To her complete surprise, Jody realized that it was *Big Boy*.

The boat manoeuvred expertly into the Ocean's Point harbour, and spluttered gently to a stop. Bob Andrews stepped out on to the deck.

He raised a hand slowly. 'Afternoon.'

'Hey, Bob.' Brice appeared beside Jody, shouldering a large bag. He was obviously on his way to the inlet, to join Craig and David. 'What brings you here?'

Bob Andrews slung a mooring rope at Brice, who caught it and wrapped it securely around a post. 'Thought I'd come and see if I could make myself useful,' he said.

Brice considered this. 'Sorry mate,' he said finally. 'We've got everything pretty much covered.' He turned to Jody and gave her a handful of leaflets. 'Would you do me a favour and post these around the harbour?'

Jody looked at the leaflets in her hand. 'CANCELLED,' she read. 'Due to a medical emergency, the *Kookaburra* tour has been cancelled until further notice.'

She checked her watch. It was one o'clock already. People would probably be gathering at the wardens' office.

'It can't be helped,' said Brice, noticing her expression. 'I know it's short notice, but no one is available to take the tour. It's a shame, because Ocean's Point could always use the money.'

Bob Andrews spoke up. 'It sounds like something I could help with.'

Brice looked surprised. 'You could?'

The owner of Golden Sands jumped down from the deck of his boat. 'Sure,' he said. 'I can read a map. I may not know much about dolphins, but I can drive a boat.'

'It's more than just a boat trip, Bob,' said Brice.

'The tourists want to hear about the wildlife as well. Do you think you know enough to keep talking for the whole tour?'

Bob Andrews looked down. After a long pause, he spoke. 'When I said I don't know much about dolphins, I meant it.'

For the first time, Jody could see that he was actually ashamed.

'I know,' he said wryly. 'People come to Golden Sands hoping to see dolphins, but what I know about wildlife you could fit on a postage stamp.' He looked up at Brice. 'I guess I'm not much use after all.'

He stared at his feet for another moment or two, before turning around and walking back towards *Big Boy*.

Dr Taylor stood up and carefully dusted himself down. 'Perhaps I could also lend a hand?' he suggested.

Jody made the necessary introductions, and everyone shook hands.

'So how do you think you could help us, Dr Taylor?' asked Brice with interest.

Dr Taylor cleared his throat modestly. 'I happen to know a thing or two about the birds along this coastline. I may be able to add something to the commentary.'

'A bird-watching trip isn't a bad idea,' Brice said thoughtfully.

Dr Taylor blushed with pride, and Bob Andrews looked alert.

Then Brice looked anxious. '*Kookaburra* is pretty temperamental. Would you really be comfortable driving her, Bob?'

Bob Andrews grinned. '*Big Boy* has a glass floor, and can take about a dozen passengers or so. What do you say?'

Jody watched Brice's face split into a large smile. 'You're on!' he exclaimed.

March 18 – morning – Dolphin Dreamer.
The Big Boy *trip went really well. Dr Taylor hasn't stopped talking about it. They actually landed at Fraser Island and took a guided walk! Bob Andrews said he'd always wanted to go there. They saw birds like pied oyster catchers and pelicans, and watched a brahminy kite dive down for fish. And Dr Taylor's prize sighting was a ground parrot – apparently it's one of the rarest birds in Australia! The high point of the trip for Bob*

Andrews was spotting a dingo sunning itself on one of the rocks by the beach, but it soon disappeared when he tried to get closer.

Dr Taylor had been humming a happy little tune ever since he'd got back from the *Big Boy* tour. He'd clearly had a fantastic time, and had made good friends with Bob Andrews. He cornered Jody that afternoon, and insisted on showing her a couple of his bird books.

'Look,' he said, pointing. 'This is a jabiru. See its marvellous red legs. Apart from its long, thin beak, I always think it resembles a black and white flamingo. And this is a brolga. A remarkable bird. We saw one nesting on one of the Fraser Island lakes. Quite astonishing. And the rainbow lorikeets – I tell you, you've never seen such colourful little birds.'

Jody was trying hard to concentrate on what Dr Taylor was telling her, but her mind kept straying to Dawn. She was on the midnight watch tonight. She checked her watch. Five hours to go.

Dr Taylor closed his book with an apologetic smile. 'I'm sorry, Jody,' he said. 'I do tend to get a little carried away with my birds, don't I? But I can see that you have something else on your mind.'

'Those birds look amazing,' Jody said honestly. 'I'm really happy that you saw them, Dr Taylor. But I can't help thinking about Dawn.'

'Quite understandable,' said Dr Taylor. 'Don't let me keep you any longer.'

And he strode back to his cabin, whistling a little tune quietly to himself.

Jody started to climb up the steps and back on to the deck. She wanted to go back to the inlet, just to check . . .

'Oh, no you don't!' Gina stood in front of Jody with her hands on her hips. 'You need some sleep, Jody. I'm not having you on any midnight watch unless you get at least four hours rest beforehand. So if I were you, I'd head straight back to your cabin and get ready for bed. Is that clear?'

Jody slowly walked back to her cabin. Brittany wasn't there. She'd grinned with delight as soon as Jody had given her Jason's message, and rushed off the boat without a second glance. Jody guessed Jason was well and truly forgiven now.

She undressed and cleaned her teeth. Her little cabin bed did look inviting, with its cool white sheets and soft pillows. She climbed in and settled down, tucking her hands behind her head and staring up at the little skylight, which still showed a clear blue patch of sky.

There was a knock at the door, and Jody's dad walked in.

'Settling down for a few hours?'

'Something like that,' said Jody.

Craig sat on the edge of Jody's bed. 'Jody, you do know that Dawn's condition isn't very hopeful, don't you?' he said after a pause.

Jody nodded, trying hard to be brave.

Craig looked down at his hands. 'We have to remember that we can't save every sick dolphin we find,' he said. 'No matter what we do, sometimes a dolphin's time is up.'

Jody was silent. She knew her dad was trying to prepare her for the worst, and it left her with a sick feeling in her stomach.

'Sleep well,' said Craig, kissing her and standing up. 'I'll call you when it's time for your watch.'

Jody stared up at the skylight again as the cabin door swung shut. Four more hours. She knew she wouldn't sleep a wink.

* * *

Somehow, the hours passed. Jody tossed and turned in the dark, and drifted into anxious dreams. One dream was so vivid that she jerked awake with a pounding heart, imagining that Dawn had died in the night.

'Are you OK?' Brittany whispered across the room. 'You were making a really funny noise.'

Jody shook her head, trying to clear it. 'Yes,' she said after a moment. 'I'm fine. It was just a dream.'

But was it? She checked her watch. It was just after eleven-thirty. She scrambled out of bed and pulled on a sweatshirt and jeans. She knew the night air would be cold.

'Good luck,' said Brittany sleepily. 'I hope Dawn's OK.'

The moonlight was bright, casting strange, long shadows across the beach. Jody met her father halfway down the sandy shore.

'How is she?' Jody asked immediately.

Craig smiled wearily. 'She's still with us,' he said. 'I don't know where she's getting the strength from. She hasn't eaten anything all day.'

'She wants to survive,' said Jody, suddenly certain of it.

Craig gave a tired chuckle. 'You might just be right,' he said. 'There's no other explanation for it.' He touched Jody lightly on the shoulder. 'David will be back in a couple of hours. Just stay with Dawn until he comes, OK? The only thing we can do for her now is keep her company.'

Jody quickly ran down to the inlet. The moon had painted the sea silver, and there was a strange hush in the air.

Dawn was lying motionless in the water. Jody held her fingers above the dolphin's blowhole, and felt only the faintest breath. But she was still breathing.

Jody settled down on the sand, and started to talk. She told Dawn about all the places they had visited on *Dolphin Dreamer*. She described the different dolphins they had worked with, and the people they had met. She talked about the different climates, and the huge variety of birds and animals they had seen. She talked about her friends back at home, about her school and her life in Florida. Somehow, she knew that Dawn was listening, and that hearing the sound of Jody's voice was soothing her. Jody felt a special bond with the sick dolphin, and promised herself fiercely that there was still hope. For as long as it took, she would keep talking.

'Talking to yourself?'

Jody jumped up when she saw David.

'Dad said you'd be at least two hours!' she said in surprise.

David checked his watch. 'Well, I don't know what time you came down here but it's two o'clock in the morning now.'

Jody couldn't believe it. How had she talked for so long? She looked at Dawn. The dolphin was as motionless as she had been at midnight, but her blowhole was still gently opening and closing. Would she pull through?

10

March 19 – morning – at the waterfront café in Ocean's Point.

Dawn lasted the night. I knew she would! I went to see her first thing this morning. Brittany was already down there with Jason, who took this morning's early watch. I couldn't believe it when I woke up and Brittany's bed was empty! I'm pleased that she's happy again. Now we just have to keep praying for Dawn.

Jody approached the inlet. It was the third time she'd visited Dawn that day. She just couldn't stay away, in case there was any change.

Brice and David were both in the water. They waved when they saw Jody.

'Any improvement?' she said hopefully.

There was a short silence, as David and Brice exchanged glances. Jody's heart sank. She had felt so positive last night that Dawn was going to improve.

'She's not getting any better, is she?' she said, biting her lip to keep it steady.

David shook his head gently. He looked tired. 'Her health was poor to start with,' he said. 'For a dolphin to battle something like this, they need to have been strong and well initially. To make things worse, this is a particularly nasty human form of pneumonia, as your dad suspected. We're running out of time, Jody.'

Jody looked at Dawn, who was lying ominously still in the enclosed inlet. Her eyes were half-closed. Even her hump seemed smaller, and her dorsal fin was flopping sadly off to one side.

David spoke again. 'It's unkind to prolong her suffering. Unless she responds within the next two hours, I'm afraid we will have to discontinue the treatment.'

'No!' Jody cried defiantly. 'We won't! We can't!' she cried as David's words sank in.

'It's not fair on Dawn, Jody,' said Brice, putting his arm around her shoulders. 'You know how cruel it is to let an animal suffer when there's no hope.'

Jody turned to him, her expression fierce. 'There *is* hope!' she insisted. 'We mustn't give up. I know Dawn can get through this!'

She turned and fled up the beach, tears blurring her eyes. She ran as fast as she could, not caring where she was going.

'Hey!'

She felt two strong arms catch her around the waist and lift her off the sand. It was her dad.

Jody burst into tears. Craig just held her and stroked her head. Jimmy and Sean stopped their games, and came over to stand quietly beside their sister. They seemed to know that this wasn't the time to play any stupid tricks.

At last, through hiccups and sniffles, Jody managed to tell her dad what David had said.

'Well!' Craig exclaimed. 'What are you worrying for? He said we still had a couple of hours to hope, didn't he? Look on the bright side, Jody!'

Jody quietened down, and concentrated on breathing steadily and calmly. 'Two hours isn't long,' she said.

'But it might just be long enough,' replied Craig.

Jody looked at her dad's crinkled blue eyes, and felt her spirits lifting a little.

Craig pointed to a picnic blanket under the trees. Mei Lin had laid out a feast of food – cold tuna, a brightly-coloured bean salad, mounds of floury white rolls and wedges of cheese. Gina and Maddie were unpacking a cool box filled with frosted bottles of lemonade. Cameron was wrestling with a coconut, which he was trying to pierce with his penknife. Jody could see that the food looked fantastic, but her stomach was rebelling. She just wasn't hungry, not with Dawn so ill.

'It's lunchtime,' Craig said encouragingly. 'Let's go and have something to eat. You'll be more use to Dawn with some food inside you, OK?'

Jody dutifully put a few bits and pieces of food on her plate. She hadn't had any breakfast because of her early start, and it was already past twelve o'clock. But the soft white rolls tasted like cotton wool and the tuna like cardboard. She ate

Mei Lin's feast!

mechanically, and thought about Dawn the whole time.

At last, her plate was empty. Jody looked up dully, and realized that Brittany was nowhere to be seen.

'Where's Brittany?' she said at last.

'Out with her *boyfriend*,' sang Jimmy wickedly.

Sean dissolved into giggles.

'She's gone snorkelling with Jason,' said Gina, passing Jody a piece of creamy white coconut. 'Those two really seem to have hit it off. I must say, I almost miss the tetchy Brittany we all know and love.'

When lunch was over, Jody felt strangely sleepy. Lulled by the swishing of the wind through the trees above her, she drifted off into an odd, dream-filled sleep. Images of pelicans, dugongs, ospreys and dolphins floated through a watery world in her mind. All the dolphins looked like Dawn.

She awoke with a start. Dawn! What time was it? How long had she been asleep?

She could see her parents at the water's edge with her brothers. Maddie and Cameron were sitting together under a tree a little further along the beach, chatting quietly. She checked her watch. It was one-thirty – over an hour and a half since she had left Dawn with David and Brice.

Jumping to her feet, she looked towards the inlet. She was too far away to see anything, so she started to run. She ran down the beach, right up to the inlet. She couldn't run fast enough. It seemed much further away than she remembered.

At last she reached it. But she couldn't ask the question. She just stared at David, who was wading out of the water towards her.

'It's OK,' said David. 'She's responding.' His face

broke into a huge grin. 'This is one tough animal, Jody. She's going to pull through.'

March 19 – morning – sitting on the sand at the inlet. I cried all over again when David told me that Dawn was going to be OK. Dawn's eyes were open, and she even clicked at me, though she was pretty weak. Somehow she'd found the strength to keep fighting. David could hardly believe it. By the evening she was starting to get restless, banging her tail from side to side and tossing her head. David wanted to keep her under observation for one more night, just in case. I found them feeding her some fish this morning. She couldn't get enough of it. Maybe chips from a greasy paper bag won't taste so nice in future!

Jody tucked away her diary and took a handful of warm sand, letting it run slowly through her fingers. They had all gathered at the inlet to watch Dawn being released back into the ocean. Brittany was there with Jason. Jimmy and Sean had built a sandcastle, and were standing on the top of it, fighting for the best view. Craig and Gina were chatting with David and Brice, and Mei Lin, Harry,

Dr Taylor, Cam and Maddie were all watching from a distance.

David turned to Jody. 'Would you do the honours?' he asked.

Jody got to her feet, her stomach tightening in anticipation. She looked at the netting which sectioned the inlet off from the rest of the sea. Carefully, she unhooked the net, and ravelled it slowly across to the other side. The way to the deep blue sea was now open. Would Dawn take it?

With a powerful beat of her tail, Dawn shot through the opening. Within moments, all they could see of her was a powerful wake, streaming after her like a long, silken ribbon. Then that, too, disappeared.

Jody felt disappointed. Was that it?

Gina came to stand beside her. 'It's a good sign, Jody,' she said encouragingly. 'It means that Dawn felt well enough to turn her back on us and return to the sea without a second glance.'

Jody walked slowly back up the beach towards *Dolphin Dreamer* with the others. Mei Lin had arranged a big celebratory lunch, and everyone was invited.

Bob Andrews was waiting for them in the harbour. He'd brought *Big Boy* back to Ocean's Point that morning, and he was full of plans that he couldn't wait to share.

'I've decided to use *Big Boy* to run tours at Golden Sands,' he announced. 'What do you think?'

'That's great!' Craig gave a genuine smile. 'Good luck to you.'

Bob Andrews waved his hand. 'I still maintain that I can only drive a boat,' he said. 'But young Dawson – remember him? It turns out that he's keen to learn more about dolphins since he found Dawn the other day. He's already learned a whole lot of impressive stuff, so I thought I'd employ him on the boat as my commentator.' Then he looked across at Dr Taylor. 'And this clever guy has provided me with some terrific notes on the birds we saw at Fraser Island. So we can run bird-watching tours on the island as well.'

Dr Taylor looked so pleased that Jody thought he might burst into tears. 'I'm honoured to have been able to help,' he stuttered.

Bob Andrews suddenly looked serious. 'But my most important decision is to start employing

147

wardens,' he said. 'It's time that we had some kind of system in place and stopped the feeding. I never want to go through that business again, and I'm pretty sure the dolphins don't either.'

'We'll drink to that,' declared Gina, raising her glass.

'A toast, then!' said Craig, rapping the side of *Dolphin Dreamer* to catch everyone's attention. 'To a new enterprise and happy dolphins.'

'To a new enterprise and happy dolphins!' everyone chorused.

And with a clink of glasses, the party went into full swing.

March 19 – siesta time – aboard Dolphin Dreamer. *Everyone's sleeping off their lunch now. Bob Andrews has gone back to Golden Sands, and the food has been cleared away. It was a fantastic party. So why don't I feel happier? I know it's selfish of me, but I really thought Dawn would have said goodbye. I sensed a connection with her, but I guess I was wrong.*

'Jody?' Sean tugged at his sister's sleeve.

'What is it?' Jody asked, putting her diary carefully down on the deck.

'There's an insect on the deck,' he said. 'We don't know what it is, and it's really huge!'

'Where . . .' Jody started to say. Then she remembered.

'Oh no,' she said, shaking her head and picking up her diary again. 'You're not going to get me a second time, OK? That's a really old joke now, Sean.'

'No, really!' Sean protested.

Jimmy came running up. 'Jody, you've got to come!' he said. 'Everyone else is asleep!'

Jody looked around. Her parents were down in their cabin, Dr Taylor was snoozing in his deckchair, and Brittany and Jason appeared to be fast asleep on the cabin roof, side by side on Brittany's towel.

Jody sighed. 'Jimmy, forget it! It was funny the first time around, but not now.'

A sudden movement caught her eye. She looked around to see the most enormous creature leap across the deck. Jimmy and Sean shrieked.

'It's a grasshopper!' Jody gasped.

The grasshopper was bright green and looked almost exactly like a leaf. Jimmy and Sean were right. It was enormous.

It paused in the middle of the deck. Then in one

flying leap, it took off and landed smack in the middle of Dr Taylor's lap.

Dr Taylor woke abruptly from his snooze. He let out a great bellow of fright, and jumped to his feet as if his shorts were on fire. 'Get it off me!' he roared.

And he leapt over the side of the boat and into the water with an enormous splash.

After a shocked silence, Jimmy and Sean collapsed into howls of laughter. Jody hurried to the side of the boat and peered into the water. 'Are you OK, Dr Taylor?' she asked anxiously.

Choking and spluttering, Dr Taylor surfaced. His face was bright red and his eyes were bulging. He'd clearly had the most terrible shock.

'Unreal!' cried Brittany from the cabin roof.

Dr Taylor bobbed around in the water, opening and shutting his mouth like a fish. At last he managed to speak. 'What was that?'

Jody was about to break the news to him that it was only a harmless grasshopper, when another splash just outside the harbour drew her attention.

A long, thin, pink and white splashed beak rose from the water. It was followed by a domed pinkish head and an unmistakable hump.

Dawn floated on the surface of the water, expelling air gently from her air hole. Then she rolled back under the water again.

Jody held her breath, and watched. Suddenly the dolphin flew up into the air in a graceful arc, flipping her tail once before plunging back into the water. She had come to say goodbye after all.

You will find lots more about dolphins on these websites:

The Whale and Dolphin Conservation Society
www.wdcs.org

International Dolphin Watch
www.idw.org

Look out for more titles in the Dolphin Diaries series:

Book 1: *Into the Blue*

Lucy Daniels

Jody McGrath's dolphin dreams are coming true! Her whole family is sailing around the world, researching dolphins – and Jody is recording all their exciting adventures in her Dolphin Diaries . . .

Jody can't believe her dolphin voyage has begun. A whole world of discovery awaits her aboard *Dolphin Dreamer*. But an unexpected passenger threatens to spoil the trip of a lifetime. And when a sudden storm puts Jody's life in danger, who can she turn to for help?

Look out for more titles in the Dolphin Diaries series:

Book 2: **Touching the Waves**

Lucy Daniels

Jody McGrath's dolphin dreams are coming true! Her whole family is sailing around the world, researching dolphins – and Jody is recording all their exciting adventures in her Dolphin Diaries . . .

The McGraths are in Key West, Florida, visiting a very special dolphin centre – with dolphin teachers! Jody loves watching the dolphins at work. But then one of the teachers goes missing . . .

Look out for more titles in the Dolphin Diaries series:

Book 6: ***Racing the Wind***

Lucy Daniels

Jody McGrath's dolphin dreams are coming true! Her whole family is sailing around the world, researching dolphins – and Jody is recording all their exciting adventures in her Dolphin Diaries ...

It's the last leg of the McGrath's journey, and Jody is looking forward to meeting the unique river dolphin, known as the boto, as she arrives in the South American rainforest. But, the beautiful boto dolphin is difficult to track down – it's even in danger of extinction! Will Jody get to make friends with the rarest Dolphin in the world ... ?

ORDER FORM